# The Truth About Horses, Friends, & My Life as a Coward

# Meet the family:

**Fancy Free . . .**
the largest horse around, with feet the size of pie pans and a brain the size of a pea. Also known as “that moose horse.”

**Sweetheart . . .**
is only sweet *in* the ring. Outside of it, she’s a terror. Loves to knock riders off under tree branches.

**Really, the Pony . . .**
a fat, furry fiend who
bites, kicks, rolls, and
runs away with pony carts.

**And me . . . the biggest weenie in Maine:**
Aims to save other
poor souls from torture
by horses.

# The Truth About Horses,
## Friends, & My Life as a Coward

by **Sarah P. Gibson**

illustrated by **Glin Dibley**

Amazon Publishing
Attn: Amazon Children's Publishing
P.O. Box 400818
Las Vegas, NV 89140
www.amazon.com/amazonchildrenspublishing



Library of Congress Cataloging-in-Publication Data
Gibson, Sarah P.
The truth about horses, friends, and my life as a coward / by Sarah P. Gibson. – 1st ed.
p. cm.
Summary: As she fearfully begins learning to ride and manage the horses she never wanted her family to own, Sophie Groves also begins to acquire friends on the Maine island she calls home.
ISBN 978-0-7614-5991-0
[1. Horses–Fiction. 2. Ponies–Fiction. 3. Horsemanship–Fiction. 4. Friendship–Fiction. 5. Family life–Maine–Fiction. 6. Maine–Fiction.] I. Title.
PZ7.G3579Tru 2008
[Fic]–dc22
2008005545

*Book design by Anahid Hamparian*
*Cover illustrations by Glin Dibley*
*Cover design by Anahid Hamparian*
*Editor: Marilyn Mark*

*To my grandfather,*
*F.W. Gibson,*
*who would have been proud*

*And, of course, to my loyal friends:*
*Really, Sweetheart & Fancy Free*

# Contents or What You're Getting Yourself Into. . . .

**Preamble or Beginning** 1

**1. Heidi and the Pony Cart or How Not to Make Friends** 3

*In which I introduce myself and warn potential horse lovers with the true story of how a girl came over to play at my house, something nasty happened, and she never returned again.*

**2. How Not to Buy a Pony or Danger in a Small Package** 10

*In which I explain how I ended up being stuck with horses in the first place and learned my first important lesson: the smaller the horse, the meaner the horse.*

**3. The Carpwells Come to Town or The Pony Meets Her Match** 20

*In which I describe the weekend visit of three gum-chewing, spur-toting "family friends," who proceeded to terrorize not only me but our good-for-nothing pony.*

**4. Melissa Maloney or The Friend Who Wouldn't Go Away** 25

*In which I discover the best friend I never had and relate how she attempts to ride the unrideable pony.*

**5. The Arabian Nightmare** or
**Don't Look a Gift Horse in the Mouth** **32**
*In which we give up on the pony and buy another horse, only to discover the true meaning of the phrase "Arabian horses are clever and nimble-footed."*

**6. The New Barn** or
**Enter Fancy Free, Horse #3** **42**
*In which, by accident, we end up with yet another horse and I get tricked into taking riding lessons against my will.*

**7. The Carpwells Ride Again** or
**Nearly Drowning the Horses** **53**
*In which I suffer through another weekend with the dangerously dynamic Carpwell trio, learn how to cling to a swimming horse, and prove yet again that I am a complete and utter weenie.*

**8. How I Learned to Ride** or
**The Sleepiest Horse in Maine** **63**
*In which I survive my first riding lesson, realize that there is such a thing as a horse that is too calm, and end up in the nerve-racking position of trying to canter while everyone is watching.*

**9. Outwitting the Tricky Beast** or
**Survival Beyond the Ring** **74**

*In which I attempt to ride our own horses, lose my best friend for the summer, try to gain another, and perceive, at last, that some things in life cannot be changed.*

**10. Try, Try Again** or
**Learning to Get Back On** **85**

*In which I am bucked off, freaked out, patched up, and forced to ride again, or have my new friend believe I am a total weenie.*

**11. The Battle with Debbie** or
**Soaring the Steel Steed** **93**

*In which I am surprised by the evil Carpwells, save my friend, get tricked into having the ride of my life, and finally stand up to Debbie . . . though she nearly kills me.*

**12. The Wild West Horse** or
**Bigger Is Not Always Better** **99**

*In which I am convinced to ride Horse #3, a horse so large I need a stepladder to mount her, and encounter the problem of having two friends who can't stand eachother.*

**13. A Visit from the Blacksmith** or **How I Lost My Common Sense** 109
*In which I talk to the farrier, try to ignore my best friend's urge to do something stupid and dangerous, watch a movie, and eventually lose my head.*

**14. Feats of Derring-Do** or **Stuck in the Muck** 115
*In which I attempt to ride the Elephant Horse outside of the ring and encounter both the joy of riding with a friend and the agony of discovering what happens when a horse can't jump.*

**15. Running Unbridled** or **The Night of the Halloween Horse** 122
*In which I almost die from fear twice in one night, commit a crime, cement a friendship, and attempt to catch an escaped "horse."*

**16. Left at Home Alone** or **One Short Ride in April** 135
*In which I learn that friends, as well as girth straps that aren't oiled regularly, are unpredictable, and admit the value of a faithful steed.*

**Epilogue** or **Ending** 145

# Preamble OR Beginning

**So, you think you love horses? Loads of people *say*** they do, especially to me. Usually, though, it's new girls at school. When they find out my family owns horses, they sit next to me at lunch and try to be nice. They munch away on their sandwiches, looking all dreamy-eyed.

"So, Sophie"—one will begin by stating the obvious—"you have horses."

I nod and keep eating.

"How many?" she will persist, and I know that even though she's sitting right beside me, she's actually far away—riding a galloping horse, usually pure white, across a field of waving grass. The sun is shining, and the wind is blowing the hair back from her face. Only I know about that rock the horse is going to trip on, or that the horse's tail is up because he is farting into the wind, or that the lovely shirt the girl is wearing will be forever after covered in horsehair and smell of sweat.

It is time to snap her out of the spell. "Two and a half," I answer.

"What?" she says, focusing her eyes on me again. "Two and a half what?"

"Horses," I answer, slurping my drink. I can see her struggling with this concept. She doesn't understand my joke. I sigh and decide to end her confusion. "Two horses and a pony," I explain.

"Oh—a pony! Is it a small one? The kind you can drive around in a cart?" she gushes.

"Well . . ." I hesitate. "We *used* to drive her around in a cart," I admit.

She falls for the bait. "Used to?" she asks, puzzled.

Now, here is where I usually tell the story of Heidi and the Pony Cart. She's bound to find out, anyway, and then avoid me. Which is fine because I want my friends to like me for me—not for my horses.

# 1

# Heidi and the Pony Cart OR How Not to Make Friends

**Heidi is the smartest girl in our class. She's actually** nice about it, though, and doesn't make a big fuss or anything. She carries around a notebook stuffed with lots of papers that keep falling out and is always scrambling around underneath her desk trying to catch them. You think she's not paying any attention, but then she'll pop up and answer a question nobody else can.

But being smart has its problems. No one really likes to hang around someone they can't understand. I didn't, either, but back when we were in third grade, our mothers decided we should play together. Why? Because we live near each other. That's the most ridiculous reason, but sometimes there's no talking to my mom. When she gets an idea into her head, you can just forget about anything else you had planned. In fact, that's how we ended up with horses in the first place—but I'll get to that later.

Anyway, I went over to Heidi's house, and she showed me her room, which was packed with books and papers and a few rotting apple cores among the piles of dirty laundry. We played an encyclopedia game that she pulled out of the piles. It was kind of boring, but I had an okay time, so I invited her over to my house the following week.

And it probably would have been fine except that my mother got one of those *oh no* kind of ideas into her head.

"Why don't you and Heidi go for a pony-cart ride?" she suggested after lunch.

"Heidi doesn't want to," I said quickly.

"Sure she does. Don't you, Heidi?" Mom asked.

"What? Oh, sure." Heidi was busy looking through our telescope at a bird. She had no idea what she had just agreed to.

"Mom—," I started, but she cut me off with a wave of her hand.

"I'll help you with the harness," she said brightly.

And that was that. We were doomed.

∩ ∩ ∩

Our pony, Really, is a Shetland, and true to her breed: she is extremely short and extremely furry. She is also knock-kneed and fat. This is because being the meanest pony around for miles (and I mean hundreds and possibly thousands), no one dares to ride her. She excels at biting, kicking, and rolling her victims. So far, no one has ever tried twice. Which leaves only the pony cart. This contraption she will tolerate, but not happily.

Catching Really is never a problem because she has a weakness for sweets, and she remained docile that fateful day of Heidi's visit—until Mom approached with the harness. Then her ears shot backward. Now, ears back mean a mad horse—the farther back, the madder. It's a scary sight to see, because somehow, when a horse's ears go back, their eyes get rounder and their teeth get larger. Really's ears lay back clear onto her neck, and I got a bad feeling in the pit of my stomach.

"Can I pet her?" Heidi asked innocently.

"Not right now," I said quickly.

Mom finished buckling on the harness and backed Really between the shafts of the pony cart, issuing instructions all the while. "Just keep a firm grip on the reins," she concluded. "And remember, you're in charge, and she knows it."

I somehow doubted that, as Really's ears hadn't moved forward so much as an inch, but I stupidly climbed in anyway. I guess Mom's optimism had made me think I could do this. Neither one of us told Heidi that this was my first time driving the pony cart without Mom in it.

"Do you want to come?" Heidi asked my mother as she sat down beside me. She was smart enough to realize this trip might be a little risky.

"No, no, I have some painting to do. You girls go and have a good time." Mom beamed. But to me she whispered, "Gramp will be watching."

Swallowing down my nervousness, I said, "Giddyup."

Really stood there, her knock-kneed legs locked.

"GET GOING!" I yelled, lifting the reins up. Really swung her head around and gave Heidi and me a disgusted look, but she started forward. I settled into the seat, feeling a small sense of accomplishment. She walked very slowly out of the barn driveway, and we turned right.

The plan was to drive around the Point. We live on an island in Maine, and my family has forever owned this piece of land that juts out into the ocean. To get to it, you have to cross a strip called the Narrows, which has a sandy beach on one side, a grassy road in the middle, and a meadow of sea grass on the other side. After the Narrows, the land rises up above sea level, and the road continues into the woods of the Point, where it meanders around in a large figure eight.

We started across the lawn, passed my grandfather's house, and headed toward the Narrows. It was sunny, and the tide was in. The seagulls were busy breaking mussel shells on the rocks, and the breeze flapped the flag on Gramp's flagpole. This I remember clearly. What happened next I also remember clearly, but why it happened will always be a mystery. One minute we were rolling along and talking; the next we were galloping, the wind whipping our hair around our faces. Really was running like sea monsters were chasing her, dragging the wildly bouncing cart down the dirt road.

"Aaaaaggghhh!" I cried. I clutched the side of the cart, and Heidi clutched me as we flew onto the Narrows. I pried one of Heidi's hands off of me and yanked on the reins, but it made no difference—there was no stopping that pony. She had the bit in her teeth—literally. Then I noticed that a large clump of seaweed, left from the last storm, was stretched across the Narrows road ahead of us, and I breathed a sigh of relief.

"She'll stop there," I yelled to Heidi above the rattling of the cart.

I was wrong. Really did not stop. But the cart did. The wheels jammed in the seaweed—that is, until the force of Really leaping over it broke them free. Then the cart—with us still clinging to it—bounced clear off the ground and straight up into the sky. For a long, long minute we were airborne, until the cart crashed back down onto the road with a *smack* that emptied out what little air was left in our lungs.

But our ride was far from over. Really continued to run—up the rise at the end of the Narrows and into the woods. Trees flashed by in a whirl of green, and branches whipped at us like angry snakes.

"Duck!" I hollered, and as we crouched down inside the cart, I stole a quick glance at Heidi. Her face was the color of spring peas, and her eyes were the size of two hard-boiled eggs.

*Can I get out now?* she mouthed at me.

"Are you crazy?" I hollered back. I knew she would break at least one bone if she tried such a stunt.

And then I looked up and saw the junction where the roads crossed—and considered jumping out myself. I desperately tried pulling on the reins, but Really ignored me while she decided which way to go herself. First she veered to the right, then to the left, and then at the very last minute, she veered again to the right. As she did, the cart rose up on one wheel. With a terrified cry, Heidi started sliding down toward the ground, and I grabbed her by the shirt. We missed a poplar tree by a foot, and the cart bounced back down onto two wheels as Really gathered speed again.

It was such a blur of fear and motion that it's hard to say how many times we zoomed around the Point, glued to the bottom of the cart in terror, before Really finally ran out of breath. She slowed to a canter and then to a trot. And the very second Really dropped to a walk, I shoved Heidi out of the cart and leaped out after her. Really jumped at the noise and flew off again, vanishing through the trees. We stood listening to the wild clatter of the cart echoing farther and farther away as we gulped in air, safe at last.

"We'd better get off the road," I said after a long moment of silence.

Heidi jumped and looked around as if expecting to see Really coming back to run her over—which, I had to admit, was a distinct possibility. We scrambled out onto the rocks and sat down. To our right lay the ocean and to the left the Narrows, my family's houses, and the rest of the Island.

"Look!" Heidi gasped, and pointed.

Emerging onto the Narrows was a teeny brown pony followed by a furiously bouncing red cart. And she was heading straight for Gramp, who was running as fast as he could down the road toward the

Point. We watched openmouthed as he dove out of the way at the very last minute. Really raced past him and leaped over the seaweed yet again. The cart flew up, then bounded down behind her on the road as she dashed across Gramp's lawn and disappeared from view.

I later found out that Mom had been out talking to our new neighbors, the Viles, when Really, wild-eyed and covered with foamy sweat, galloped up the driveway. All talking ceased abruptly as Really raced past them and around the house three times, until she finally stopped under the apple tree in the front yard.

I think my mother was, for once, speechless. And our neighbors were never very friendly after that. Neither was Heidi. After Gramp fetched us home, my mother offered Heidi ice cream, petting the new kittens, and even going sailing, but Heidi stayed quiet. She didn't blink a lot, either, as I recall. We never played together again.

∩ ∩ ∩

There is usually a long silence when I finish this story, and then the girl mumbles an excuse, grabs her lunch, and scrambles away. Sometime later, I will see her talking to Heidi, who, bless her, doesn't like to talk about it but does confirm that the story is true.

And that's how I save another poor soul from torture by horses.

## 2

# How Not to Buy a Pony OR Danger in a Small Package

**How is it possible to own horses and not like them,** you ask? Well, when you've seen what I've seen, it's *very* possible. And if you're planning on learning to ride or spending any time around these devious creatures, you need to understand what you're getting yourself into. In order for you to get the whole picture, though, I guess I had better begin at the beginning. . . .

∩ ∩ ∩

Mom got the wacky idea to buy a horse when I was too young to object. I was only five at the time that Mom decided Sharon, my eight-year-old sister, should learn to ride. Most people would have just signed their child up for riding lessons. But not my mother. No, she had to *own* one. Whatever put the idea into her head, I don't know and probably never will. My mother is an artist and a stubborn one at that. This means that if anyone objects to her loopy ideas—usually my poor dad—she just says she's being "creative" and gets away with her eccentricity (that's a nice way of saying craziness).

But this time Dad protested.

"I love horses. I always wanted a horse. The girls want a horse," Mom pleaded. My sister stood beside her, hands clasped, eyes filling with tears.

I added, *"Please, Dad!"* It was a line I'd later regret, but it worked. Dad sighed and headed for the cookie jar, which in our house meant he was giving in.

Because my sister and I were still small, Mom decided a pony would be best. Had she consulted knowledgeable people, she would have discovered lesson number one in the world of horses: "The smaller they are, the meaner they are," and thus that ponies are trouble with a capital *T*. but that is not Mom's way. She always plunges ahead into what she wants and learns as she goes. Unfortunately, so does the rest of the family.

So, one spring day Mom drove Sharon and me to the pony farm. The owner led us into his field full of ponies. And there was Really, dozing sweetly in the sun. She was pregnant at the time and just stood there, round as a pumpkin and blinking sleepily while we petted her, stuck our fingers up her nose, and pulled her tail.

"Isn't she sweet?" Mom gushed.

We bought her.

Dad was not happy when he got home from work and heard the news. "You bought a pregnant pony? I agreed to one horse, not two!" he bellowed.

"I know, I know," my mother said, "but she's so nice, and it will be a good experience for the kids," she added. "They'll be able to ride together when Sophie gets old enough."

My father shook his head and trudged off to eat more cookies.

During the next week, he and Gramp built a fence that began at one of the old fish shacks (which became our first barn) and encircled our large yard. The only problem was that the garage was on the other side of what was now the pony pen, so my father had to walk through the pen every morning and evening on his way to and from his car. However, this did not seem like much of an issue at the time.

After the fence was completed and we had gone to town and bought shavings, grain, and hay, Really was finally delivered. My sister just about peed in her pants she was so excited. She loved to feed and brush Really. She couldn't ride her because of the unborn foal, but my parents bought a used saddle and bridle, and Sharon practiced riding on an old sawhorse that Mom set up.

And then one morning two months later, we came outside and there was a pure white filly (that's a girl pony) standing beside Really. Mom entered the paddock first. She gave Really a little pat on the neck and bent to pet the baby. That's when we met the *real* Really—she immediately leaned forward and bit Mom on the bum.

"Ow!" Mom cried, standing up and grasping her bottom.

Really's ears lay straight back against her head, and she bared her teeth. My mother dashed for the fence, and Really dashed after her. Mom leaped over the gate as nimbly as a steeplechase runner and collapsed beside us. Really snorted in triumph and trotted back to her foal.

"Maybe," Mom said between gasps for breath, "we should leave them alone for a few days."

My sister and I nodded. We weren't about to argue.

My mother consulted with the vet when he came out later that morning. He said the meanness would probably be temporary; Really was only being an overprotective mother with her firstborn.

Unfortunately, Mom forgot to warn my father, who had been away on a business trip. We were in the kitchen that afternoon when we heard the yelling.

"Your father!" Mom gasped, and we all ran outside to see Really chasing him through the paddock. Dad was running full tilt toward us, clutching his briefcase and waving his suit bag.

He almost made it to the gate when he slipped on some fresh pony manure and fell. My mother ran to open the gate as Dad leaped up. Using his briefcase as a shield, he backed slowly out of the paddock, and Mom slammed the gate closed behind him. Really grabbed hold of his suit bag and shook it viciously.

"What happened to *her*?" my father asked in a shaky voice. His suit was covered in grass and pony by-products. My mother quickly pointed to the foal and explained what the vet had said.

My father muttered something under his breath and stomped off to take a shower. Mom baked a fresh batch of cookies and, after dark, snuck into the pasture and retrieved the suit bag.

∩ ∩ ∩

We named the foal Truly, as in Really and Truly. She was sweet and playful and fun to watch, and for almost a year that's all we did, because Really didn't allow us to do anything else. When my poor father got home from work, he either had to run full speed through the pasture or walk along the shore from the garage. He claims this was the reason that he finally gave up his banking job on the Mainland and returned to lobstering with Gramp, but I suspect it was because he hated wearing a suit.

By spring, Truly was big enough to wean, and Mom decided to sell her so that Really would revert to her old sweet self. Problem was, nobody wanted Truly. Finally, the Bowdens, who owned a large dairy farm just across from us on the Mainland, offered to take her off our hands. They had some nieces who came to visit in the summers, and they figured a pony would be fun.

"Now, girls," Mom explained to us, "there's no need to mention Really's . . . uh . . . little problem. Every horse is different, and Truly will probably turn out very sweet."

"Sure, Mom." We nodded. We hated to see Truly go, but to be honest, I was sick of not being able to use our swing set, which was located inside the paddock.

So the Bowden boys, Mark and Philip, came to get Truly. They were large, well-muscled teenagers used to handling ornery cows.

"Our pony's a little overprotective of her foal," Mom warned them.

Philip nodded calmly. He and Mark carried two lead ropes and a small halter. They climbed over the fence and walked across the pasture. My sister and I scrambled up on the fence for a good view and, more importantly, to get out of harm's way.

Really's ears went flat back as they approached, and she stood in front of Truly, legs braced.

"Now there, pony," Mark said, placing his hand on

her neck. Philip walked around the other side. He was just about to touch Truly when Really bit Mark, whipped around, and kicked at Philip.

Hollering out some swear words I had never heard before, Mark ran for the fence and took it in one leap. Philip followed right behind, with Really thundering after him, teeth bared. The boys lay stunned on the ground for a whole minute.

Mom pulled the first aid ointment out of her pocket and handed it to Mark. He eyed her suspiciously as he got up and dusted himself off.

"A *little* overprotective, Mrs. Groves?" he asked, rubbing some ointment on the red teeth marks on his arm.

My mother looked sheepish, but only for a moment. "You boys manage those cows all day long. I didn't think a little pony would be much of a challenge for guys as strong and large as you."

Now, put that way, the Bowden boys *had* to go back into that paddock or their reputation around town would be shot. But they sure didn't want to. They looked at each other sideways and had a little whispered conversation. Then they looked at Really, who stood watching over Truly with a don't-you-dare-come-near-me expression on her face.

At last they picked up the lead rope and the halter and headed back in. This time Mom scrambled up on the fence with us. Slowly they spread out, and each boy approached from a different side. Really whipped her head back and forth, but she couldn't keep her eye on both of them at the same time. Mark reached out a hand, and when she turned to bite him, Philip looped the lead rope around her neck. Really turned to snap at him, but before she could close her teeth, he pulled back, smacked her lightly on the nose, threw his arm around her neck, and held her in a headlock.

She snorted in surprise, and so did we. Really tried to move, but she was no match for the well-muscled Philip. In the meantime, Mark, speaking softly and slowly, slipped the halter on Truly and led her out of the pasture, feeding her bits of carrot as he went. Once the gate was closed, Philip released Really, who dashed to the fence and neighed wildly for Truly. Philip walked calmly by her and climbed out. Then they loaded Truly into the trailer and drove away.

∩ ∩ ∩

That was our first lesson in pony management, taught to us by cow owners, but very valuable nonetheless. We all developed a new respect for the Bowden boys that day.

Of course, they didn't have any real use for a pony, so they just kept Truly with their cows, and she grew up thinking she was a cow, coming in to be milked at five with the rest. It was a strange existence, but I think she was happy.

Really moped around for a week. We felt sorry for her and fed her sugar and carrots through the fence. She was even too sad to chase my father through the pasture.

"Well," my mother said, sighing with relief, "now we can finally start to ride her."

It was the beginning of a battle that lasted a year, before my mother admitted defeat. (In fact, we had long deemed her unrideable when Melissa Maloney showed up, but I'm getting ahead of myself.)

Anyway, when Really was in a good mood, she would tolerate being ridden. The problem was, you never knew when her good mood was going to end. Therefore, at any moment, you had to be prepared to jump off and run. My mother bought Sharon teeth-proof riding boots, a hard hat, and a small whip called a crop, but nothing helped.

As for me, I wouldn't even sit on that beast no matter what Mom said. I was simply not that stupid and never would be. So, after my sister was scraped against the fence for the umpteenth time, my mother temporarily gave up the idea of our riding Really and instead announced happily that we would train her to pull a cart.

"Horses should only be raised to be eaten," my father muttered as he threw away the new boat brochures he had been collecting.

Soon after, a brand-new cherry red pony cart arrived. Mom wheeled it into the pasture and let it sit. "This way she will get used to it," she explained to us.

Really ignored it.

It was summertime, and Mom stopped painting and threw herself into the project of training the pony. Using lots of sugar cubes, she added a little bit more harness each day, and then she worked at lunging Really (running her around on a long lead line). Mom led her up to the cart, day after day, and rattled and banged it until Really no longer rolled her eyes in fear. Then she backed Really between the shafts and slowly hooked her to the cart. She walked Really up and down the pasture until the pony was used to the strange sound behind her. Finally, Mom carefully climbed in and drove her around in a circle.

After a few days of practice, Mom stopped by the gate, where my sister and I sat watching. "Get in," she commanded. I choked on the piece of grass I was chewing. Was she crazy? I shook my head vehemently. Sharon hopped down and walked over to the cart.

"Just sit on the edge; you can jump right out if anything happens," Mom coaxed me.

My sister climbed in smoothed down her shorts, and smiled at me. *Chicken*, she mouthed.

That did it.

I climbed down from the fence, perched myself carefully on the seat of the cart, and Mom started off. It was kind of peaceful, jouncing along in the sun with the bees humming around us and the barn swallows swooping overhead. Then Mom made a small mistake: she dropped one of the reins to swat at a fly.

Really saw her chance. She reared up and took off running.

"Jump!" Mom hollered, and we all leaped out. I fell flat on my face but sprung right up and sprinted for the fence, followed closely by my sister.

Really ran around and around the pasture, reins flying, cart bouncing, eyes wild and white, ears back. Mom cornered her at last and got her calmed down and unhitched.

I thought that would be the end of the cart, but if there is one thing more stubborn than a Shetland pony, it is my mother. The next morning, she started at the beginning and went through the steps all over again, only this time she asked the Bowden boys to come over and sit in the cart with her. There was no running this time. Really could barely pull the pony cart with them sitting in it.

So, for a while, either Philip or Mark would go driving with us, and people on the Island got used to seeing the pony cart crammed full of bodies with a sign hooked onto the back that read "Slow please!"

That's how Mom tamed the wild pony to the cart . . . well, at least for a while. . . .

# 3

# The Carpwells Come to Town OR The Pony Meets Her Match

**After Really ran away with Heidi and me, the pony** cart sat in a corner of the barn and gathered dust. Even my mother had to admit defeat. That is, until the Carpwells came for a visit one weekend in May.

Now, if there was one family that could strike terror into my heart, it was the Carpwells. There were three kids in the family, and all of them were chock full of pent-up, electrifying energy. Because I was the youngest, and arguably the most timid, they appeared to me as daring and wicked as outlaws.

First there was Debbie, the eldest. She was tall and wiry with a bush of blonde hair that she tried unsuccessfully to control with barrettes. She was fourteen and ruled over us underlings with an iron fist. No one dared to disobey "Queen Deborah" (which we called her behind her back, of course).

Except maybe Judd, the Second in Command. He was one year younger than Debbie and had coal-black hair and one black eyebrow that stretched across both eyes. He never came to our house without a broken bone or stitches or both. Judd could shimmy up any tree on the Point, whip apples clear across our field, ride standing up in the saddle with one hand holding the reins (the other being in a cast), and hold his breath underwater longer than anyone else I ever knew.

Lori was the youngest, and frightening in her own way. One year younger than my sister, she was sort of her friend. Sharon was no crybaby and was in fact so ruthless herself that once, when we were arguing, she slammed a door on my finger, then locked it and walked away, calmly ignoring my screams. So when I say that beside Lori, Sharon appeared as meek as a newborn kitten, you will see that Lori was a force to be reckoned with.

Lori was small and thin, but when Debbie ordered her to obey, she disobeyed and often paid the price—by being locked in the attic or being made to do all the dishes herself (Debbie was always in charge if our parents went out). Lori stubbornly did the punishment, but she never gave in. She was a true rebel at heart.

The Carpwells, as far as I could see, feared nothing. And, since they owned horses on their farm up in northern Maine, they certainly weren't afraid of a barrel-stomached, knock-kneed, undersized bundle of fur with long teeth. So when they saw the dust-covered pony cart sitting in a corner of the barn, they immediately decided they wanted to use it. My sister made a few weak protests, but she was silenced with a wave of Queen Deborah's hand.

"Catch the pony," she ordered imperiously.

I scrambled up on the fence silently, deciding it would be a good idea to get out of the way. But Really allowed herself to be caught and harnessed, mainly because of the sugar lumps Lori kept feeding her.

Judd hauled the pony cart out of the barn, and Debbie hitched her up. I thought I could see a gleam in Really's eye as she swung around to look at the cart. Mom said Really was afraid of the cart, but she didn't look scared to me.

As the oldest, Debbie got the middle seat and the reins. Judd and Sharon sat on either side of her, and Lori and I were supposed to cram in and sit on the floor. But I flat-out refused to do it.

Now, to refuse a direct order from Queen Deborah was a courageous act for me, but getting in that pony cart was far worse, I figured.

There was a moment of awed silence.

"Why not?" Debbie demanded, but I was beyond speech at that point.

"She's afraid of the pony cart," my sister explained.

"Oh, is that all," said Debbie. "Well, sit on the side bar and then you can jump off if you want to."

It was a royal command, and I had to obey or suffer terrible consequences because Debbie was officially "in charge." Our parents were all out on the boat, and the gang couldn't go anywhere without me. So it was everyone, not just Debbie, glaring at me.

I crumbled into submission, meekly climbed down from the fence and, trembling, walked over to the pony cart. The minute my bottom touched the edge of the bar, Debbie said, "Gee-up," and Really reared straight up into the air. I yelped in fright and clutched the cart. Really came down and leaped forward in the harness, but with all our weight, the cart only rolled forward about a foot. Really stopped dead in her tracks, stunned.

Debbie said, "Gee-up," again, but Really locked

her knees and refused to budge. I breathed a sigh of relief. Once Really assumed that position it was impossible to get her to move unless she wanted to, so it looked like the pony-cart ride was over.

Debbie slapped the harness reins down on Really's back. Really flinched but remained stock-still. Debbie's face turned a furious shade of red.

"Get out, Judd," she commanded. Judd leaped out and without any further instruction went forward and grasped Really's bridle. Then he calmly jerked her head to one side. This threw Really off balance for a moment, and the minute her weight shifted, Judd hauled her head forward. Her body followed and Really stumbled, completely surprised, into a walk. Judd jumped back into the cart, and Sharon and I exchanged glances as we absorbed this interesting lesson in pony handling.

To say that I enjoyed that pony-cart ride, cramped and balanced on the edge of the cart seat, would not be true, but I can honestly say that I enjoyed it more than Really. Debbie made her tow us all over the Island and even up and down the hills on the west end. Really was covered in lather and sweat when we finally returned and was so exhausted that she didn't even try to bite Lori when she led her out to the field.

The whole next day she remained unusually docile. The Carpwells petted, brushed, and led her around. Luckily for Really, they decided against riding her, as Debbie and Judd were too big, and Lori spent most of the day hiding after she nailed Debbie in the head with a rotten apple.

"I think she's sweet," Lori said, hugging Really good-bye on Sunday. Sharon and I looked at each other and shrugged. Maybe it was true that if you show horses you're the boss, they will obey you.

The Carpwells pulled away, waving. I sighed in the same half relief and half regret I always felt as their visits ended. They were like a carnival ride, scary yet exhilarating and something you couldn't do every day. Absently, I petted Really on the neck, and she whipped around and chomped my arm. I screamed and ran for the fence with Really pounding after me, her hot breath searing my back. I dove through the gate to safety, and Really stopped, looked at me with complete and utter disdain, and then walked off.

Yup, she was boss—and we both knew it.

# 4

# Melissa Maloney OR The Friend Who Wouldn't Go Away

**I never had a best friend until Melissa Maloney** moved in up the street. School was on the Mainland, and most of the girls were from "in town." They hung out together, led by a stuck-up blonde named Susan, and looked down their noses at us "Islanders." There weren't very many of us until Uncle George got a contract from the state to build a bridge from the Island to the Mainland.

Once you could drive to the Mainland, people started buying up land and building houses, and suddenly there were lots more kids on the Island. It was the summer before fourth grade when Melissa's family built their house near the top of our mile-long road. Our moms met and then immediately arranged for us to play together. Melissa arrived dressed in pink. She stood half a head shorter than me, had blue eyes the size of a puppy dog's, and long brown hair swept back into a perfect ponytail. I looked her over and knew right away that she liked to play with dolls and dream about horses.

And, indeed, Melissa's first words to me were, "Wow, you have a horse!"

Yup, I'd guessed right. However, I thought with

grim satisfaction, she looked like she'd be an easy one to scare off.

"Yeah, a half a one," I said resignedly as I led the way to the barn. "And not the better half," I muttered under my breath, but Melissa didn't hear that part.

"Oh, a pony—I get it." Melissa laughed. She stopped to pick a handful of grass and then approached the fence. "She's beautiful," she breathed as she leaned against the fence. Which gives meaning to the phrase "beauty is in the eyes of the beholder," because I couldn't see anything that even remotely resembled beautiful.

It was early summer, and the ground was too soft to let Really out into the field, so she stood on top of her personally created manure mound in the center of the paddock, as proud as a pig and about as fat. She had rolled in the mud, and it was caked on different parts of her coat. Winter hair was coming out in tufts all over her body, and her mane lay matted against her neck. It was a warm day, and Really stood baking in the sun with her head lowered slightly, mouth open, a vacant expression in her round brown eyes.

"Let's feed her," Melissa suggested. She started to climb over the fence, but I stopped her. Mom did at least have some rules about restraining total strangers from getting too close. And I was glad she did, because I certainly wasn't going inside that paddock.

"Against the rules," I said.

"Oh," she said, disappointed.

"Want to see the barn?" I offered instead.

"Sure!" Melissa brightened up again.

Inside, I showed her the saddle, the bridle, the cart harness, and Really's stall.

'"You know," I said innocently, "if you really want to feed her, you can stick around and help me clean the barn."

"Sure! What should I do?" Melissa asked.

I sat in the dusty pony cart while Melissa proceeded to muck out Really's stall, spread down fresh wood chips, fill the water bucket, drop down a bale of hay from the loft, and measure grain into Really's feed bucket.

"It must be fun—being able to ride whenever you want," Melissa said as she struggled with the wheelbarrow.

I mumbled something while pretending to cough. I wasn't about to let it slip that I didn't ride.

"Do you ride her on the beach?" Melissa asked as she flaked out the hay.

"Sometimes," I allowed.

When she finished, Melissa came over and sat down beside me. Her new white sneakers were now brown and smelly. I had to admire her determination. Most girls usually quit before finishing.

"Can I ride sometime?" she asked me.

"Ever ridden before?" I inquired.

"Oh yeah; I had lessons at camp," Melissa said confidently.

Now, camp horses, as a general rule, are half-dead creatures that you could put a Tasmanian devil onto and they wouldn't spook. Riding Really was an entirely different kind of sport, and I didn't have the heart to do that to someone who had just cheerfully cleaned the barn for me.

"Let's bring her in to eat," I said and hopped off the cart. I told Melissa to stay put (because I knew she'd be safe there) and went down to the gate, where Really was waiting expectantly. Keeping as far away from her as I could, I opened the gate. Really clambered up the ramp to her stall. I locked her door, and then Melissa and I leaned over the door watching her munch away happily, head buried in her grain bucket.

"Look, Melissa," I confessed, "they forgot to tell us the second part of this pony's name when we bought her. Honestly, she is *Really Mean*, and the truth is, no one rides her. She bites, kicks, and rolls."

"Oh, yeah?" Melissa pondered this for a while. "Well, could I *try* to ride her?"

Some people, I thought to myself, don't know when to take no for an answer.

"I guess so." I shrugged.

"Tomorrow?" Melissa insisted, and I shrugged again. Well, no one could say I hadn't warned her.

When I told Sharon later that night, she couldn't believe it, either. "She's crazy," Sharon said, shaking her head.

We both decided it was better not to mention this plan to Mom and Dad. Fortunately, Dad and Gramp were out hauling lobster traps, and Mom was engrossed in her painting. But Sharon was right there to watch when Melissa showed up the next afternoon, and she helped Melissa saddle the pony. Really's ears lay straight back against her head when Sharon put the saddle on her back, but Melissa ignored that—or didn't know what it meant. She held on to the bridle while Sharon tightened the girth, which barely fit because Really was so fat from lack of exercise. Then Sharon led her into the paddock, where Melissa mounted and took the reins.

Sharon and I sat up on the corner of the fence under the big pine tree. "Should have brought popcorn!" My sister grinned. She had a meaner streak than me. I was already feeling sorry for Melissa.

Melissa said "Gee-up," and Really began to walk calmly around the ring. But when Melissa turned to smile and wave, Really whipped around sideways and banged her into the fence.

"Oof!" Melissa cried, dropping to the ground.

Really turned and ran for the gate.

Melissa got up, the smile wiped clean off her face.

"You okay?" I called as I hopped down to help her.

"Yes," Melissa said between clenched teeth.

"Well, you tried," I consoled her.

But Melissa strode straight past me to the pony, gathered up the reins, and got back on.

"Oh," I said, and scurried back to the fence. Melissa whipped Really's head around, and off they started again.

Really rolled one eye backward as if sizing up her opponent. Sharon and I exchanged a silent glance. We knew what that look meant. Suddenly Really bolted into a canter, raced around the ring in a small circle, and then stopped dead in the center, front legs braced. Melissa sailed overhead and landed face-first on the manure mound. Really ran back to the gate again.

"Ew!" Sharon and I said together.

Melissa got up, wiped her face off on one sleeve, and marched toward the gate.

"I don't believe it!" said Sharon as Melissa

mounted once again. Even Really seemed surprised.

But she recovered.

Before Melissa could gather up the reins, Really turned around, trotted up to the far end of the paddock, and stopped. Her knees buckled, and she started sinking toward the ground.

"Jump!" Sharon hollered. "She's gonna roll!"

Melissa jumped clear, rolled away, and stood up. Then she got back on as soon as Really stood up again.

Sharon and I sat speechless.

On the next few tries, Really smashed Melissa's leg along the fence. She whipped around in a tight circle six or seven times, tried to bite Melissa on the leg, bucked, cantered in a zigzag up the ring, and then stopped dead again. Melissa fell off at least six more times before she finally gave up and limped toward us. Her long brown hair was pulled out of her ponytail and spiked all over her head. She was covered in mud and manure, and her pink shirt was half unbuttoned.

*"Geez Louise!"* Melissa said, gasping for air. "That is one REALLY MEAN pony."

Sharon laughed and left.

I hopped down and faced Melissa. "You're okay, Melissa Maloney," I said with admiration. We grinned at each other. Then we led the sweating pony up the ramp and unsaddled her. Melissa gave her an apple, though Really certainly didn't deserve it. She stood munching while Melissa brushed her, clearly enjoying the fact that she had won the battle.

"What do you want to do now?" I asked, glad to

finally have a friend who could truly understand how horrible horses were.

"How about trying out that pony cart?" Melissa suggested.

I groaned and shook my head.

# 5

# The Arabian Nightmare OR Don't Look a Gift Horse in the Mouth

**Even though Melissa joined the list of those who** had been bested by Really, she still continued to come hang around the barn with me and babble on about riding. Which gave my mother the harebrained idea that the solution to the problem was to get another horse.

"Another?" My father choked on his dinner. "That pony is a snot-nosed, diabolical, fur-covered fiend into which we pour money—and you want another?"

"I agree Really's a little . . . difficult." My mother hesitated for a mere second, then rushed on. "That's why we need a calmer animal, one that will be a good influence. Plus, we already have the barn." It was, in fact, a pieced-together old fish shack, but my mother ignored that fact. "And the paddock, so it shouldn't be much money."

My mother had an ability to make wacky ideas appear to be good sense. My father had figured this out, however, and would never have agreed to this latest scheme, except that the Carpwells were selling a horse at a bargain price (according to my mom), and he couldn't say no to my insistent mother, my pleading sister, *and* old family friends. He finally caved in under all the pressure, and Sweetheart arrived one weekend in August before I entered fifth grade.

Sweetheart was fourteen hands, which meant that, technically, she was only a very large pony, but she looked plenty big to me. She had been a camp horse before the Carpwells bought her, so she was used to children crawling all over her, and she stood calmly and sweetly in the paddock—hence her name.

Mr. Carpwell unloaded her tack, cheerfully said a quick good-bye, as he had to mow hay that weekend, and drove off with the horse van.

"Wow, she's beautiful," Sharon said, completely ignoring the fact that Sweetheart's back dipped down in a U-shaped sway. "Makes her comfortable to ride," Mom reasoned. Sweetheart also had a growth under her neck the size of an orange that the vet called a goiter. "He says that neither condition affects her at all," Mom said airily. "And it made her cheap to buy," she added for my father's benefit.

Sharon brushed Sweetheart all over while Mom inspected the saddle and bridle that had come with her. Sweetheart arched her neck when Sharon brushed it and closed her eyes in enjoyment. I have to admit that despite her flaws, she did present a pretty picture: she was white from head to hoof, with large, round brown eyes that looked curiously at everything when Sharon wasn't brushing her neck. Her pink nostrils flared as she sniffed at her new surroundings, but otherwise she stood quietly.

She looked so peaceful that even I was tempted to hop off the fence and feed her sugar. But I didn't, of course.

"She's pure Arabian," Mom explained to us. She'd bought a book about the breed and now considered herself an expert. "It says that they can be a little spirited but," she added quickly when she saw my smile fade, "she is sixteen—that's middle-aged in horse years—and very used to children riding her."

My mother spoke confidently, as usual, and she only faltered a little when she unpacked Sweetheart's bridle. Now, most horses have a bridle with a small snaffle bit, the part that goes into their mouth. If you pull on the reins, the bit moves and makes them uncomfortable, and they stop. That is the theory, anyway. But horses that have been ridden by a lot of silly camp kids who know nothing about riding and pull too hard on the bit learn to ignore it and won't stop. So a harder and often larger bit must be used.

Sweetheart's bit was a half-inch piece of metal with a large hump in the middle and an extra bit of chain that went under her chin. It looked like the bit you'd use to ride a bucking bronco in a rodeo.

"Well!" said Mom picking it up. "*This* should stop her," she said cheerfully as she slipped the bit into Sweetheart's mouth.

Sharon rode her, since everyone knew there was no way I was moving off that fence. Really poked her head through the paddock gate and watched curiously to see what the new horse would do.

Around and around they went, with Mom in the center shouting out instructions. First they walked, then they trotted, and finally they cantered. Sweetheart obeyed every instruction perfectly and without a moment's hesitation. Even I was impressed.

"Sophie, do you want to try?" Mom called to me.

"No!" I quickly answered. She had that bit for a reason, and I was still being cautious.

So Sharon brushed her down, and then we let her out into the field with Really. After a little nose touching Really tried to bite her, and Sweetheart lashed out a hoof that caught Really square in her stomach. Then Sweetheart turned and walked to the middle of the pasture, where the best grass was. After a surprised minute, Really followed meekly, and from that moment on, Sweetheart was in charge.

Mom and Sharon talked nonstop through dinner, raving on about the wondrous traits of the magnificent Sweetheart.

"I mean, the book is completely wrong," Mom said, waving a fork at Dad. "Spirited, indeed! Why, she's gentle as a lamb."

"And as white and pretty, too," my sister added dreamily.

"What's *that*?" my father suddenly interrupted, pointing.

We all turned and looked out the picture window toward the barn. Every twenty seconds or so, a yellow light cut through the darkness, making it look as though lightning were flashing inside the barn.

"I don't know!" my mother said. She leaped up from the table, and we all ran outside. When we got to the barn, however, it was dark and quiet. The only sound was Sweetheart and Really munching away on their nightly hay.

"Strange," my father commented.

We went back to the house and cleared the table. My father loaded the dishwasher, while my sister and I washed the pans, and my mother wiped the table.

Suddenly Mom threw down the sponge and dashed outside. She returned in a minute, and without saying a word to us, grabbed the tape from the cupboard and dashed away again.

When Mom finally reappeared, she explained the mystery. "It was Sweetheart—the light switch is right next to her stall, and she's been flicking it on and off for fun. When we went to investigate, she must have heard us coming and stopped. But I caught her the second time and taped it off," Mom said, laughing. "What a clever horse," she added proudly.

Little did we know how clever.

∩ ∩ ∩

Wild horses could not have kept Melissa away for long, and sure enough, she showed up the next morning to watch Sharon ride the new horse. She perched on the fence beside me.

My sister rode around the ring, sitting very tall and proud on Sweetheart and looking very smug. "Let Melissa have a turn," I called out. Sharon glared at me, but with Mom there, there was little she could do. So she slid off and let Melissa get on.

Melissa grinned ear to ear as she rode around the ring, stopping only to stick out her tongue at Really, who stood watching from between the rails of the paddock gate.

After ten minutes Sharon turned to me, and with a mean little smile, called out, "Give Sophie a turn." I tried to kick her, but she scooted away. "You do want to ride, don't you?" Sharon asked sweetly, knowing full well I was scared to death but didn't want to admit it in front of Melissa.

"Come on; it's fun!" Melissa called.

"She's very gentle," Mom reassured me.

I shook my head emphatically. It was early days yet—I would wait and see.

But Sweetheart continued to behave.

"I think we can ride her outside the ring," Mom announced during dinner the following week.

"Really?" Sharon cried.

"No—Sweetheart," my father joked, and we all groaned and ignored him.

"Yes, I think she's calm and gentle, and you have a good seat and nice control of the reins," my mother said.

My sister puffed up proudly. I rolled my eyes up at the ceiling. There would be no living with her after this compliment.

I called Melissa to tell her the news.

"Outside the ring?" Melissa gasped. "When?"

"Saturday morning," I said. I didn't officially invite her to come over and watch, because I knew she would show up anyway. Melissa didn't worry about small details like being polite.

"Are you going to ride her, too?" she asked.

"No way," I said.

"But Sophie, you'll miss all the fun!"

I wanted to say if that was what she considered fun, then I preferred a boring life. But I didn't say it. Because the truth was, even for me—a complete weenie—doing dangerous things with a friend *was* better than being bored all alone.

Saturday morning dawned sunny and warm, a last burst of good weather before summer ended and school began. Melissa arrived promptly at nine. Sharon rode Sweetheart around the ring for a few minutes. Then Mom opened the gate to the outside world and stood by it, issuing instructions.

"Ride down past Gramp's house, across the Narrows, and up the hill. Make sure you stop there, turn around, and come back."

My sister nodded.

There was a pine tree at the top of the grassy knoll that marked the end of the Narrows. Melissa and I ran down along the beach to it. We climbed up into the pine tree and sat on the lowest branch to watch.

We could see my mother walking with Sharon and Sweetheart up to Gramp's house. Gramp and his friend Bob Estabrook were outside tinkering on the old sawmill.

Sharon left Mom behind and headed across the lawn toward us. Sweetheart's mane and tail flowed in the morning breeze, the seagulls swirled overhead, and the incoming tide lapped lazily at the beach.

"Oh, I wish it were me." Melissa sighed, and for a moment I almost wished it, too.

They came up the hill and strolled past us. Sharon waved and headed for the trees. Following instructions, she turned Sweetheart around to walk home.

In the twinkling of an eye (namely Sweetheart's), everything changed. The minute Sweetheart's head faced the barn, her neck arched, her tail swung up, and she left the ground in a giant leap, running straight for home.

"Help!" Sharon screeched, clutching onto

Sweetheart's neck. Melissa and I gasped as Sweetheart thundered toward us, then suddenly veered sideways in a beautifully coordinated move that brought her right beneath our branch.

Sweetheart kept running, but Sharon hit the limb with a meaty thud and fell straight down to the ground. Melissa and I landed beside her, knocked off by the impact.

I looked up in time to see Sweetheart dashing across the Narrows, feet and head high, mane tossing in the wind, reins flapping wildly. She streaked by an astonished audience and headed home to the barn.

Melissa and I helped Sharon sit up so she could catch her breath. Gramp and Bob arrived first in Gramp's truck.

"You okay?" Gramp asked Sharon, who had recovered enough to start blubbering.

"Well," said Bob, leaning down, "she's crying—that's a good sign."

"There, there," Gramp said, patting her on the shoulder.

"Pshaw—a little fall ain't nothing," Bob said kindly. "Why, I had a horse step on my hand when I was your age and lost part of my finger. Now that hurt!" Bob held up his left hand, and sure enough, his pinkie ended at the first knuckle.

*"Geez Louise!"* Melissa gasped.

My sister sobbed even harder.

Fortunately, Mom arrived at that moment. Dad had stayed behind to catch Sweetheart.

"I just don't understand it," Mom said as she hugged and comforted my sister. "Sweetheart didn't act as though anything spooked her."

"Oh, horses are like that," Bob casually informed us. "They always speed up when it's time to go home."

And that was how we learned the lesson of "tire 'em out and hang on tight when you turn for home." We also now knew why Sweetheart had that big, hard bit—it was the only hope a rider had of trying to stop her.

∩ ∩ ∩

Yup, Sweetheart was a completely different horse outside the ring. She also had a seemingly never-ending supply of tricks for trying to get out of riding. When we saddled her, she would take a breath and hold it while we tightened the girth. Then she'd release her breath and the girth would loosen, so that when the rider mounted her, the saddle would slide down under her stomach, and the rider would end up on the ground, wondering what happened.

Once we got used to this trick, Sweetheart developed a cough when we led her out of the barn. It sounded like she was gasping for her last breath. At first, we worried because of her neck goiter. The vet came out for a visit and checked her over. He listened to her heart and her breathing and then gave her a long look in the eye, until Sweetheart finally had to look away.

"That goiter isn't bothering her at all. She's fit as a fiddle and a clever, clever girl," the vet pronounced with a fond pat on Sweetheart's neck.

After the cough, the limp began. Mom examined her hoof and then had Sharon walk her around in circles. Sweetheart's downfall was that if you walked her long enough, she would get tired and switch to limping on another leg.

"Aha!" my mother would cry and give the okay for Sharon to mount.

I had to admire my spunky sister. She kept riding Sweetheart over to the Point, even though Sweetheart had a million ways of knocking her off on the way home. We discovered that the book had indeed been correct in saying that Arabians are "intelligent and very nimble on their feet."

But for all that, Sweetheart wasn't mean-spirited like Really, and she was always a perfect "sweetheart" in the ring. She just enjoyed the challenge of trying to outsmart my sister, and when she managed to dump Sharon, Sweetheart knew that she had won the game for the day. Sweetheart would always dash back home and then stand quietly outside her stall, sides heaving. And my mother would look out the window, throw down her paintbrush, and holler, "Not again!"

But Sweetheart never bit or kicked or rolled, and after a while my sister grew better at ducking and hanging on. I still refused to do more than tickle Sweetheart's nose while standing safely outside the gate of her stall. However, by the end of fall, even I was forced to declare Sweetheart "an okay horse."

# 6

# The New Barn OR Enter Fancy Free, Horse #3

**A Maine winter is always long and cold, but the** winter after we bought Sweetheart was particularly bad, with lots of snow and ice and flesh-freezing temperatures. The water pipe to the barn froze, and we had to lug buckets of water from the house twice a day. The soggy wood chips and the manure congealed daily into large frozen lumps the size of tractor tires. Dad showed me how to use the axe to break them up so I could stack them in the wheelbarrow, bully my way outside into the wind, and dump them before coming back in to spread fresh chips down.

The barn roof was old and leaky, and in one storm, part of it tore off, and we had to nail on new tar paper and shingles. My mother held down the tar paper while my father hammered, and I handed up the shingles. My horse-loving sister had entered eighth grade and was conveniently off at a disgusting giggle-and-kiss party.

That left the three of us shivering in the freezing wind along with Sweetheart and Really, who watched the whole process with trembling interest. It was so cold that my hands went numb despite my down gloves, and I could hardly keep a grip on the shingles. When we finally finished, Mom and I struggled to blanket the two horses, because the wind coming in off the ocean was blowing freezing spray in through the cracks of the rickety shack.

"We need a new barn," my mother announced when we were finally inside and huddled around the woodstove with mugs of hot chocolate.

"What we need is to sell those beasts," my father muttered as ice dripped from his mustache into his cup.

My mother looked hurt. "But they're family," she said.

"Okay, okay," said my father. "But we'll have to build the barn ourselves. We can't afford a contractor."

"Of course we will. Right, Sophie?" Mom beamed at me.

I buried myself in my book, not answering. It sounded more like unpaid slavery to me.

And I was right. At the first hint of spring, every weekend became an agony of endless toil.

First we cleared brush and burned it. Then we measured and sank the Sonotubes that would hold the frame. Then Dad, Gramp, and Bob Estabrook laid the foundation beams. This took the whole weekend because Gramp and Bob kept stopping to have coffee, and that usually led to a story or two. The following weekend, Dad told them we didn't need their help, so it was only the four of us pounding nail after nail after nail. The frame slowly went up.

By the beginning of June the frame was finished, but we were all exhausted, and each of us sported at least one purple fingernail from a missed hammer hit. For once I didn't want the summer vacation to begin, since school was the only place I was allowed to sit down for five minutes. And my sister, who supposedly adored horses, kept trying to weasel out of the project so she could go hang out with her goofy friends. Even Melissa, gung ho to begin with, was finding excuses not to drop by anymore.

Finally, one Saturday morning, my mother threw down her hammer and marched inside to the phone. Uncle George arrived later that day and stood surveying the unfinished barn.

"Not bad," he said, plucking a piece of grass and chewing on it.

"How long to finish it, George?" my mother asked grimly. Uncle George was a contractor, so he was sure to know.

"Oh, at the rate you're going, maybe by Halloween. More likely Thanksgiving." Uncle George shrugged. "But don't worry, it should be done by the time winter really sets in."

"Halloween! Thanksgiving!" my mother cried. "George—this can't continue. I haven't gotten any painting done, and I have two portraits to finish."

Uncle George took off his hat and scratched at the bald spot on his head. He eyeballed Mom, his younger sister, who had two tears conveniently welling up in her eyes.

"I'll make you a deal," he offered. "I'll get a crew out here to finish the barn—if you'll board a horse for my foreman. He's been after me to build him a barn so he can buy a horse for his daughter. Frankly, I don't think he has enough land for a horse, and I don't even know if his daughter wants a horse, plus—"

"Of course we can board a horse!" Mom interrupted.

"What's one more?" she cried, too relieved to listen to the rest of what Uncle George had to say.

*"What's one more?"* my father roared when he found out. "I go to town to get some nails, and I come home to find out you've added another horse to the collection! Do you know what grain costs? Wood chips? Why, a horse eats a half a bale of hay per day in the winter, and that adds up to—"

"Ed!" my mother said sharply. "George has promised to have the barn finished in time for your fishing vacation." Now that was getting Dad where it counted. He lived for the annual trip up to Nova Scotia with his fishing buddies. Why he'd want to spend his vacation fishing when he spent almost half a year on the water hauling lobster traps was beyond me, but he did.

"Oh," my father spluttered. "Well, I suppose . . ." His voice trailed off. He turned and headed inside for the cookie jar, and we knew then that another horse would soon be arriving.

So, in between swimming and sailing lessons, Sharon and Melissa and I joined Sweetheart and Really in watching the new barn being finished. And then, late in July when the barn was finally ready, the boarder horse arrived. The van pulled up early one evening, and my father opened the gate to the paddock. The man backed the trailer in, and he and my father went around and undid the bolts of the ramp.

Out backed the largest horse any of us had ever seen. Enormous muscles rippled under her tan skin, and she swished a five-foot-long black tail around impatiently. The minute she was free of the trailer, she tossed her head and jerked the lead line out of the man's hand like it was dental floss. Then she trotted around the ring, each black hoof making a mark in the dirt the size of a pie pan.

Nobody spoke for a full minute.

"She's a Western Buckskin, and her name's Fancy Free," the man said finally, "'cause she doesn't like to be tied. See that mark over her left eye? Well, when she was young, a tree branch fell on her and she got spooked. So never raise your arm quickly or she'll bolt, and never tie her head neither."

Since none of us were capable of replying, the man continued. "She's trained to ride English and Western but prefers Western. She's good as gold, will follow you around like a dog, can trot for miles at a time. Watch the canter, though. She's a bit stiff-legged."

He strolled to the trailer and unloaded her tack onto the fence. "Any questions? No? Well, enjoy," he said, then hopped into the cab of the truck and drove away with a cheery wave.

*"Sally!"* my father hissed between clenched teeth.

"Oh my," Mom replied, at a complete loss for words.

∩ ∩ ∩

I called Melissa the minute we had coaxed that elephant of a horse into the barn and given her two buckets of water, one bucket of grain, an entire bale of hay, and six apples.

"Just how tall is she?" Melissa asked.

"Mom says she must be at least eighteen hands."

"You have all the luck." Melissa sighed.

"Are you nuts?" I cried. "One wrong move and I'll lose all my toes or fingers just like old Bob Estabrook!"

Melissa ignored my protests as she usually did.

"I'll be down first thing tomorrow morning," she promised. I shook my head as I hung up. I couldn't decide whether I should admire Melissa's complete lack of fear, or worry because she didn't appear to have one bit of common sense.

Downstairs my parents were arguing, and I joined Sharon at the top of the stairs to listen.

"We cannot board that horse! She is way too big and far too dangerous. Who will be able to handle her, for goodness sake?" my father cried.

"She's not our horse," my mother reminded him. "She's Roy Doughty's, and his daughter is supposed to be coming down to ride and care for her."

"His daughter—ride that? You need a stepladder just to say hello!" my father continued.

"Now, Ed," my mother soothed, "his daughter is in high school and is probably used to handling horses. Besides, the man said the horse is well-trained, and she went very obediently into the barn tonight."

But there was no soothing my father this time, and he stormed off into the bedroom muttering unprintable phrases about four-legged creatures.

∩ ∩ ∩

Melissa arrived at the "butt-crack o'dawn," as Gramp always said, and ate breakfast with us. Dad had recovered to the point where he was whistling when he left to haul his traps. Mom smiled in relief and then went to let the horses out into the paddock. Usually this was our chore, but today she ordered us to stay inside. We all lined up at the picture window to watch. First Really trotted out, and then Sweetheart. After a minute, a huge tan body filled the door of the new barn and thundered down the ramp. Even from our distance you could see the boards shaking under her immense weight.

*"Geez Louise!"* Melissa whispered, both hands pressed against the glass. "She could have been a knight's warhorse! Riding her would be like advancing on a tank, like flying through space, like—"

"Who says *you're* riding her?" my sister interrupted drily.

"Oh, right," said Melissa, disappointed.

I was only too relieved that someone else had to ride her. Even my sister didn't seem eager to get too close.

Roy Doughty's truck pulled into the driveway, and we went out to say hello. My mother came from the barn to greet him as well.

"Hulloo, Mrs. Groves," Roy called. The passenger door opened, and out stepped one of the fattest girls I'd ever seen. She was round as a penny and the color of one, too, from her copper hair to her freckles to the rusty brown tracksuit she wore.

"This is Ginger," Roy said, introducing us.

Now, we had all heard about Roy Doughty's daughter. She lived with her mother over in New Hampshire and only came to visit on weekends. We'd heard she was plump; we'd heard she was spoiled; we'd heard she was mean. But though she was standing there with a very sour expression on her face, I couldn't help feeling sorry for her. I mean, I wasn't exactly a string bean myself, plus I wasn't about to have a go at riding a moose.

"Hi," we said.

"Hi," she said back, and there was an awkward pause.

"Well, come and see Fancy," Mom said brightly, and everyone turned and headed around the corner of the house to the paddock.

"There she is, honey," Roy said, pointing to Fancy, who stood in the middle of the ring. Sweetheart and Really stood in her shade.

Ginger's eyebrows shot up. Her freckles popped out as her face paled to a shade lighter than white. Fancy trotted up to the fence and hung her head over it. Only Melissa, naturally, dared to go up and offer her an apple.

It was gone in one chomp.

"Well, Ginger, let's find her tack and then—" Roy stopped as Ginger whispered something into his ear.

"Oh . . . okay, sweetie." Roy straightened up. "We can't stay today. Tell you what, we'll come back tomorrow," Roy said to my mother.

Ginger had already rolled her way to the car and climbed in, without so much as a glance at any of us. She slammed the door.

"I'll ring you," Roy called, and they drove off.

And that was the end of Ginger's riding.

It came out later that Roy, knowing nothing at all about horses, had bought Fancy as a surprise. He had hoped to help his daughter get into shape in a fun way, and he'd gotten a good deal on Fancy from a friend.

But one look at Fancy had scared Ginger into getting her father to send her to a nutrition summer camp, where she had a great time swimming and hiking, lost weight, and met some new friends. A happy ending to the story, my mother said.

But not for us—we were stuck with Fancy.

"Roy gave her to us for free," Mom informed Dad after Roy called.

Dad pushed away his plate. "It's a wonder I don't have an ulcer." He groaned. "Why do you always have to tell me these things at the dinner table?"

"Did I tell you that I have three commissions from the Spencer family?" Mom deftly changed the subject. The Spencers were a wealthy summer family, so this was encouraging news, and Dad perked up.

"Good for you!" he said.

Mom smiled proudly, then added, "So, we can afford to keep Fancy." Before Dad could say anything, she rushed on. "She's actually quite gentle despite her size, and if we keep her, the girls will be able to ride together."

My father's fork stopped halfway to his mouth.

"Ride? Together? Sophie won't even put her foot in the stirrup! What are you talking about?" he demanded.

My mother turned to smile at me. Now I stopped eating, too. I felt a terrible sense of foreboding.

She wagged a finger at me. "I've been thinking about that. To be fair, Sophie's had some bad experiences. She just needs some good ones to replace them and perhaps some proper instruction. I've had a word with Agnes Maloney, who agreed that riding lessons are just the thing."

"Riding lessons?" I cried, dropping my fork in horror.

"More money," Dad complained.

"Why *her* and not *me*?" my sister wailed.

∩ ∩ ∩

I flat-out refused. I hadn't ever asked for horses; I didn't want to ride; and I could care less about getting near anything that could maim me for life in ten seconds or less.

Mom came up to my room and sat on my bed.

"Sophie—look, I understand you're scared. But riding can be fun; horses can be your friends. They aren't all like Really. Look how nice Sweetheart is," she pointed out.

"In the ring," I muttered, still reading my book.

"And Fancy is large, I admit, but she's turning out to be quite gentle," Mom added.

"No one's tried to ride her yet," I pointed out.

"Melissa will be going with you to riding lessons," Mom said.

And that turned out to be the problem.

Melissa was wildly excited about riding lessons, but because her mother worked in town, my mom had agreed to drive us. So if I refused to go, then Melissa wouldn't be able to go, either.

"That's blackmail!" I accused my mother.

Mom laughed. "Nonsense—it's just the way it is." She shrugged. "You have to decide what's more important: being stubborn or making your best friend happy," she said.

"Please, please, please," Melissa begged that night on the phone. "We'll be in a ring, with a real instructor. I'll be with you. What could happen?"

"A lot could happen, and you know it!"

I sulked but I knew I was beaten. I just couldn't say no.

And so it was: Melissa and I would take riding lessons on the Mainland every Wednesday afternoon. For the sake of friendship, I had doomed myself to a tragic fate.

# 7

# The Carpwells Ride Again OR Nearly Drowning the Horses

**Before I had to endure the agony of riding lessons,** however, I had to survive Labor Day weekend with the Carpwells. Was there no end to my misery? And I didn't have Melissa as an ally. She had gone camping with her family. I had pleaded to be allowed to go, and so had Melissa. Even she paled at the description of the Carpwell clan, but her mother was determined to make it a "family" holiday. So poor Melissa was stuck with her dorky younger brother, and I was forced to face the Carpwells without her support.

My sister wasn't too happy, either, as she had wanted to go to a beach party up-island. We sat together on the fence on Saturday morning, watching the horses crop the last of the summer grass. Fancy pawed at a patch of dirt with one huge hoof, causing a cloud of dust to swirl up into the air.

"Well, they might be able to boss Really, and they might know all of Sweetheart's tricks, but I don't think they're going to be able to order Fancy around," Sharon said.

"Nope," I agreed.

So far, Sharon had only dared to ride "Pie-Pan Foot," as we called her, in the ring. The big horse was very docile and did *exactly* what you asked of her. Which meant that if you turned her toward the fence and asked her to walk, she would plow right into it. Even Mom was forced to admit that Fancy was sweet but not all that bright. Still, it made a welcome change from Sweetheart's tricks and Really's nastiness.

We heard a car pull into the drive, and I gritted my teeth. Within minutes Debbie sauntered up in her stately manner, flanked by Judd, who sported a new white bandage over his right eye, and Lori, small and grungy as ever.

"What happened to you?" Sharon asked Judd.

"Oh, Debbie and I had a rock fight—and I lost," Judd said, waving a hand absently at his head. "Five stitches. Hey, is that the new horse?" he asked, pointing.

At the sound of voices, Really's head swung up. When she spied the Carpwells, she shot off to the farthest corner of the pasture, where she stood watching us warily. Sweetheart and Fancy exchanged nervous glances and followed suit. The Carpwells didn't seem to notice this less-than-warm welcome.

"Whew, it's hot," Debbie said, moving into the shade of the pine tree. "What are we going to do?" she asked with a disdainful look at the house and the yard.

"Hey, the tide's in," Lori said. "Let's go swimming."

"Yeah, we'll take the horses!" Judd suggested.

*"What?"* I cried before I could stop myself.

They ignored me as usual.

"I'll ride the new horse," Debbie announced.

Only Judd complained. "Ah—no fair; I'll ride her down, and you can ride her back," he said.

"I'm oldest; I ride both ways," Debbie declared. She swung away from the fence to face him, a dangerous look on her face.

Judd clenched his hands into fists and stepped toward Debbie. "Yeah, says who?" he challenged.

"I'm not sure anyone can ride her," Sharon said quickly.

"Why not?" Debbie demanded.

"Because we haven't ridden her outside of the ring yet." Sharon's voice squeaked under Debbie's steely glare.

"We'll ask," Debbie announced and set off for the house. We fell in line behind her, me being last, as usual.

Our parents were grouped around the patio table drinking coffee, eating doughnuts, and laughing. Judd dove for the doughnuts while Debbie did the talking.

"We want to go swimming. It's really hot and we thought the horses might like a cooldown."

"Sounds like fun," boomed Mr. Carpwell. As a former football player, he was another Carpwell no one ever argued with, and Debbie smiled triumphantly.

I looked at my parents in desperation, but they were obviously too busy socializing to have taken in what this meant.

"But nobody rides Really, and Sweetheart always dumps Sharon and races for home, and Fancy hasn't been ridden outside of the ring—ever," I blurted out.

The grown-ups stopped talking, and Debbie shot me a black look that meant my life—for that weekend, at least—was over.

"I'd be surprised if Lori couldn't manage the

pony; Judd knows all of Sweetheart's old tricks; and I bet our Debbie can handle that big horse," Mrs. Carpwell interjected. She smiled at us all.

My heart sank.

"Well." My mother appeared to be thinking. "Riding bareback can be tricky. And Sophie. . . ." Her voice trailed off, and I felt myself growing red from my hair to my sandals. It was one thing to be a weenie but quite another for everyone to be reminded of it.

"Sophie will ride with Judd," Mrs. Carpwell announced firmly. "Sally, you worry too much. Kids will be kids; you gotta let 'em live a little."

My mother nodded slowly, and not daring to utter another word, I was led away like a condemned prisoner. My heart was already pounding, and I felt sick to my stomach. As soon as we were around the corner, Debbie hauled off and punched me in the arm.

"Ow!" I yelped in pain.

"You almost ruined it!" Debbie snarled, pressing her face close to mine.

My throat closed up, and I stopped breathing.

"Aw, leave her alone," Judd said, stepping between us.

I managed to take a breath as Debbie stomped away.

"Come on," Judd said. "You ride behind me."

*Ride! Bareback! No way!* But I didn't dare to say so out loud, since I needed Judd's protection from Debbie.

The horses, clued in to Really's nervousness, needed a handful of sugar lumps before they allowed themselves to be caught and bridled.

Debbie climbed on the fence and slithered onto Fancy's back. After a minute or two of riding the horse around the ring, she ordered Sharon to climb up behind her. "She's gentle as a kitten," Debbie declared.

I hoped so, looking at Sharon's pale face. I don't know who I felt more sorry for, her or me. But Sharon is made of tougher stuff than I, so with only one worried look at me, she took Debbie's hand and scrambled onto Fancy's back.

Then Lori mounted Really, who rolled her eyes but did nothing because, more than she hated being ridden, she hated being left behind.

"Come on, Sophie," said Judd.

"I'll open the gate," I said, stalling for time. I let everyone out and then latched the gate closed. "I'll walk," I announced quickly. "You guys go ahead."

Debbie swung Fancy around to face me. "Listen, you worms-for-brains twerp, Mom said you ride with Judd or else we'll *all* be in trouble!"

I swallowed nervously. What was worse: being beaten up by Debbie or riding Sweetheart? Quivering, I walked over to Judd, who hauled me up behind him with one yank of his beefy arm. I immediately latched my arms around his waist.

Satisfied, Debbie turned Fancy around and led us down the road to the beach. Judd was sticky with sweat already, and Sweetheart's fur itched my bare legs. Really trotted by us, shaking her head and giving little bucks that caused Lori to swear and jerk back on the reins.

Gramp waved at us from the driveway, where he was scraping barnacles off the bottom of his old skiff.

I kept waiting for the inevitable disaster and for the ground to rush up and meet my face, but nothing happened. We clopped along in the sun, the breeze fanning back my hair, and I relaxed a little. Maybe I would be able to slide off before we got into the water.

We reached the beach, but before I could even scrunch my eyes closed, Debbie plunged Fancy right in, and Sweetheart lunged after her. Deeper and deeper we went until the cold water swirled up around my legs in tiny whirlpools.

"Hang on tight!" Judd yelled. As if he needed to say anything—I was already clinging to him so tightly, I didn't know how he could breathe. But Judd never noticed mere physical details.

Down, down, down we sank until I floated up off of Sweetheart's back, and only her head appeared above the water. She lunged, and I plopped back down again. We rushed through the water chasing after Fancy, faster and faster, legs pumping, hooves flashing up out of the depths, and water flying everywhere. And then, just as suddenly, we clambered back up onto the beach and stood, water dripping, sides heaving, and everyone brushing wet hair out of their faces.

I had survived!

"Yee-haw!" Judd yelled, startling the horses. "Let's do it again!" he cried and plunged back in.

"Yee-haw!"

Was that *me* yelling? It was, and I did it again. This was fun! 'Round and 'round we went, chasing Fancy and then Really, the horses lunging and blowing and so excited that they eventually all pooped in the water—and then the game became how to avoid the floating balls of manure.

"Ahhh—yuck! Go left, go left!" I cried. Judd turned Sweetheart, and I could see that his now-sopping bandage had half come off, exposing black stitches and a thin red line against the white skin of his forehead.

"Judd—your bandage!" I yelled above the splashing, and Judd reached up with one hand and ripped it clean off. A few drops of blood appeared, and my mouth dropped open in horror, but Judd just laughed and whooped, and away we went again.

At last we all stood dripping and gasping for breath on the beach. Even Really's head drooped. We slid off the horses and walked them up to the grassy knoll, where we let them crop the grass with their bridles on. Normally this was not allowed, but the Carpwells were never ones to follow rules. Plus, the horses did deserve a treat.

I was as pumped up as if I had ridden on twenty scary rides at the Clam Festival. Even Sharon was grinning from ear to ear. But the Carpwells merely flopped down on the grass and sighed as if they did this kind of thing every day. Which, come to think of it, they probably did.

"What should we do now?" asked Lori.

*Rest* is the word that came to my mind, but they didn't appear to even be tired.

"There's a pretty good breeze," Judd said, holding a hand up to the wind. "We could go sailing," he suggested.

Now, if there was one thing that terrified me more than riding, it was whipping around in a small tippy boat in deep, murky green water. All three of the Carpwells jumped up, and my happy bubble popped.

Debbie, as befitted her position, stepped on Sharon's back to mount Fancy and then pulled my sister up behind her. Judd swung onto Sweetheart and yanked me up. Lori hopped on Really, who immediately whipped her head around to try and bite Lori's leg and knocked into Fancy, who shied and banged against Sweetheart, who jumped and jerked the reins out of Judd's hands.

And Sweetheart was off, cantering down the hill and stretching into a full gallop as we crossed the Narrows. Beach and sky flashed by in a blue and beige blur. I clung to Judd, but I could feel us slipping sideways, until suddenly there was no horse—only air—and we crashed together into a huge clump of damp, salty seaweed.

It happened so fast that I just lay there stunned. Judd sat up and calmly spat out some seaweed.

"You okay, Sophie?" he asked, but I was too busy trying to breathe to be able to answer.

The others arrived, and they rolled me over and felt my arms and legs.

"No broken bones," Judd said expertly.

"No blood," Lori added.

"Sit up!" Debbie ordered.

I sat up. I was trying not to cry and clenched my teeth, but the tears spilled out anyway.

Having witnessed the whole scene from his driveway, Gramp dutifully arrived with the truck, and I flung myself into his arms. He drove me home, where Mom detached herself from the Carpwells long enough to look for bruises, give me ice cream, and settle me on the chaise lounge in the shade.

It was inevitable that I'd be discovered.

"You left us with all the work of washing down the horses and the bridles!" Lori complained.

"There's nothing wrong with you," Judd said, completely perplexed as to why anyone would prefer lying down to going sailing with them.

"You're the biggest weenie I've ever met," Debbie pronounced in a disgusted tone, and off they trooped, dragging my sister along with them.

I didn't care. So what if I was a weenie? I'd much rather be a live weenie than a dead hero.

Mrs. Carpwell declared that I should be forced to

get back on that horse, but my mother shook her head. One look at my face and she knew I'd had enough. She and Melissa might still get me to take riding lessons, but I made a solemn vow that day to never ride *our* horses ever again.

# 8

# How I Learned to Ride OR The Sleepiest Horse in Maine

**My mother took Melissa and me to buy jodhpurs,** and for Melissa, riding boots as well. I already had a pair, much worn from mucking out stalls rather than riding. I would have preferred to keep it that way, but I couldn't back out of my promise—even after Sweetheart dumped me. We had started sixth grade that year, and our new middle school, filled with kids all larger and older, made me nervous. Melissa was my only friend, and I needed an ally.

But on Wednesday, "the big day," I hardly noticed what went on in school. After the last bell, we changed in the locker room so we would be ready when Mom picked us up. Melissa sauntered down the hall, showing off her new boots. I scuffled along after her, feeling more than a little stupid in my scruffy, crusty boots which, though I had scrubbed them, still smelled strongly of horse poop.

It was just my luck that Susan—and her clique—were still at school. She wrinkled her nose when she saw us and laughed. Melissa lifted her own nose in the air and sashayed past. I looked the other way and tried to ignore the giggles and whispers that followed us.

But not everyone laughed. As we waited at the curb, Rachel, who was also waiting to be picked up, confessed, "I wish I could take riding lessons." She was new at the school and obviously had not been warned off us yet.

"The only thing better would be owning one," she added, with a sideways glance at me.

I sighed. She had seemed so nice and sensible.

"Yes, it is delightful to have horses," I agreed, and Melissa's eyebrows shot up in surprise.

I ignored her. "Except that our insurance has gone up dreadfully since the accident."

"Accident?" Rachel took the bait.

"Well, *accidents*, really, but the last one was the one that did it. I was out riding, and my horse saw a snake and spooked. She ran me under a tree branch, and as I fell off, my foot got caught in the stirrup, and I was dragged. And then . . . well, you don't need to hear those details. The scar is healing really well, though, and my therapist thought that riding lessons might help me deal with the post-accident trauma.

"Melissa's been nice enough to agree to go with me, although"—I leaned in close to Rachel, whose brown eyes were solidly round by now—"I heard there was also an accident at the riding stable. They say the girl needed plastic surgery," I whispered confidentially.

I straightened up. "Do you want to come over sometime and see my horses?" I offered with a smile.

"There's my mom. I have to go," Rachel said quickly and hurried off.

I waited to laugh until she was out of sight.

"You're wicked," Melissa said, shaking her head.

I did feel a twinge of guilt at being mean but defended myself anyway. "It was for her own good, Melissa, and you know it. She should thank me for saving her from the awful fate that I am about to face," I added with emphasis.

Mom was late as usual, so my stomach was doing backflips by the time she finally arrived, green paint still on her fingers.

"The light was so good for painting this afternoon," she apologized as we sped down the back road toward the farm with the stables. We arrived exactly at 3:30, and Melissa and I quickly piled out of the car.

Mom grabbed my arm. "Do you want me to stay?" she asked quietly.

I hesitated. After all, I was eleven years old. But there were times when having your mother around was comforting, and I certainly needed comfort at that moment. I quickly nodded yes and then hurried after Melissa into a huge roofed ring covered with wood chips and swirling sawdust. The ends of the ring were open, and along the sides ran stalls for the horses.

Mr. Richards, our instructor, lined up all six victims—I mean riders—and inspected us. He looked like a circus director in his black jodhpurs and boots. He was tall and dark, and his hair was slicked back with some sort of hair gel that smelled minty.

He strutted back and forth in front of us as he explained the rules. Every week we would be assigned a horse. We then had to bring our horse out of the stall to the cross ties, saddle and bridle him (or her), and then lead the horse into the ring, mount, and line up in the center. Afterward we were responsible for unsaddling, unbridling, brushing, and returning our horse to the stall. Then we were to wipe down the tack and return it to the tack room.

"Any questions?" he asked.

"Do we have to muck out the stalls as well?" I asked, already resenting having to pay to do what was really his work. It seemed like my trick was being played back on me.

"Only if you want to," Mr. Richards replied with a cool glance that didn't bode well for my future. I cursed myself and my big mouth.

"Can we feed them?" Melissa asked.

"Apples or carrots only—if you wish to bring some," Mr. Richards answered.

"Naturally," I murmured to Melissa under my breath.

"Today your horses are all saddled and bridled," he continued, and my stomach flipped over again as he led us to the edge of the ring, where six horses stood patiently. One by one, he sent us off, until only I was left.

"You have Pete," he said, laying a heavy hand on my shoulder. "Pete's old and sweet, so be gentle with him," he added with a slight squeeze.

Had he sensed my terror? Did he know about my problem?

I took a deep breath and approached Pete, a candidate for the glue factory if there ever was one. His black coat was dull and rough, and his square head hung down. He was breathing heavily, and his eyes were shut.

"Hullo, Pete," I said softly, and he opened one eye, glanced at me wearily, and shut it again. I gathered up the reins and tugged slightly to get him moving.

He shuffled after me into the ring. My heart pounded with every step we took.

*Don't be silly*, I told myself. *He's too old and sleepy to cause any trouble*. But, of course, the problem with horses is that you never truly know. Even Pete, if he was stung by a bee, could wake up and easily buck me off. However, I seemed to be the only one aware of this fact, because all the other girls looked blissful as they led their horses into the ring.

I swung myself up on Pete, and he snorted and moved to the center of the ring without any instruction from me. Then I searched for all the possible objects that would be dangerous to be bucked onto, rolled over on, or shoved against.

Melissa came up beside me, mounted on a pretty palomino who certainly appeared to have more energy than Pete. "He needs a can of Red Bull," Melissa suggested, looking at Pete's lowered head.

"I like him just the way he is," I said staunchly.

But after twenty minutes of digging my heels into Pete's sides and yanking up on the reins to get him to walk, I began to wonder. It was taking so much of my energy just to keep him moving forward that I didn't have time to be nervous.

"When are we going to canter?" asked a girl who couldn't even hold her reins correctly or keep her feet in the stirrups. I rolled my eyes at Melissa. This nincompoop had no idea what trouble she was asking for.

"Not for a few weeks yet." Mr. Richards smiled at her enthusiasm. I heaved a sigh of relief.

"We need to learn how to walk and trot with perfect control before we begin to canter," he explained. "Sophie, tighten up those reins," he added.

I pulled Pete's head up yet again, but I don't think he was ever one hundred percent awake during the entire lesson.

"Bye, Pete," I said when I had finally cleaned up and put everything away.

His only reply was a gentle snore.

And then it was over. I had made it through alive and whole, I suddenly realized on the way to the car. Sweet relief flooded over me, and I listened patiently to Melissa's raptures on the way home. The lesson had been wonderful; her horse was wonderful; the stable was wonderful; Mr. Richards was wonderful.

"Yeah, if you like the greasy type," I joked. Melissa elbowed me, and we laughed.

"How did *you* like the lesson?" Mom asked me after we'd dropped Melissa off.

"It was okay," I said carefully. I didn't want to appear too positive and encourage another nutty Mom idea, like signing me up for horse camp or something.

∩ ∩ ∩

The next week I wasn't quite as worried, but there were still butterflies doing jumping jacks in my stomach when Mom dropped us off. *What horse would I have this week?* I wondered nervously.

Mr. Richards lined us up and assigned the horses. He gave Melissa a tall, thin gray horse who neighed when she approached. Once again I was last.

"And you have Pete," Mr. Richards said.

"Oh," I said. *Pete again?*

Pete was asleep when I approached him and stayed that way through the whole lesson, though he managed to blink himself awake to eat the apple I offered at the end.

"Bummer you had Rip van Winkle again," Melissa said as we walked to the car, where Mom was waiting.

"I like him," I said with a shrug. "He's nice and quiet and predictable."

But I have to admit I was a little disappointed when Mr. Richards assigned him to me on the third week. And, by the fourth week, when we were learning to post when trotting, I began to get tired of trying to rise up and down off the saddle while pulling Pete's head off the ground. I was also beginning to suspect a possible secret collaboration between the polished Mr. Richards and my artful mother.

"I don't know what you mean, dear," my mother protested, oh-so-innocently, when I questioned her. "If you want to ride a different horse, then why don't you just ask?"

At the end of the fifth class, I lost my patience and screwed up my courage. After feeding Pete his apple, I approached Mr. Richards. "Do you think I might be able to ride a different horse next week?" I asked.

He beamed at me. "Certainly, certainly," he said. I smiled back and found myself actually looking forward to the next riding lesson.

The following week, Mr. Richards lined us up and, as usual, assigned me last.

"There he is," he said, leading me over. You could tell it was a different horse because his coat was gray instead of black, but it was dull and rough and his large square head hung down, eyes closed, mouth slightly open. Mr. Richards slapped him on the back, and he snorted awake. "This is Repeat—Pete's brother," he said, and left.

"Hullo, Repeat." I sighed.

"Doesn't look like much of an improvement," Melissa whispered to me in the ring.

"It's Pete's brother," I explained.

"I can see the family resemblance," Melissa commented drily.

I was contemplating how to ask for a horse that was a little more awake (but not too awake) when Mr. Richards announced that today we would try cantering.

Suddenly Repeat seemed the perfect horse for me.

Mr. Richards gave us a five-minute lecture on the finer points of cantering, which I couldn't hear because of the blood pounding in my ears, and then he ordered Tracy to the side of the ring. I slumped in my saddle in temporary relief.

Tracy was the most enthusiastic, if not the best rider, among us, and she certainly had the snappiest horse—a little brown mare the size of a pony with (in my expert opinion) the temperament of one as well. Tracy nudged her horse, and they walked around the ring.

"Okay, turn her head slightly to the wall, and when you're ready, give her the signal," Mr. Richards ordered.

Tracy turned her horse's head, clucked her tongue, and the horse leaped into a canter so quickly, Tracy lurched backward in the saddle.

"Hold the reins!" Mr. Richards hollered, but it was too late. Tracy had done a complete backflip off the rump of her horse and landed in a heap in the wood chips.

We all gasped, but Mr. Richards calmly strolled over to help Tracy up and dust her off. He talked to her quietly while one of the stable workers caught the horse and led her back over. Tracy shook her head, and Mr. Richards had her pat the horse as he talked with her some more. Finally he helped her mount and walked her back to the center of the ring, where she sniffled and avoided looking at the rest of us.

I was impressed both with her and with Mr. Richards. *What did he say to get her back on that horse?* I wondered.

Mr. Richards studied the group for a long minute. He looked like he was getting ready to lecture us again. Well, at least we wouldn't have to try cantering for a while.

"Your turn, Sophie," he said quietly.

"What?" Had I heard him right? He gave me a thumbs-up sign and jerked his head toward the outer ring. Repeat ambled out. My mouth went dry, and my tongue stuck to the roof of it. Mr. Richards joined me at the side of the ring.

"I can't do this," I managed to whisper, fear overriding my pride.

Mr. Richards stroked Repeat's neck. "Listen, Sophie, you have to do this. Everyone needs to see it done correctly and successfully. You have the best seat, the best grip on the reins, and the most knowledge of horses."

Was that true? Pride flowed through me.

"Plus, the most dependable horse in the bunch," Mr. Richards added, and my fragile ego deflated. "Repeat is just like Pete. He won't try anything," Mr. Richards reassured me. He had a very soothing voice. "Your worst problem will be keeping him going," he added and then walked away, leaving me alone with a dozing Repeat and everyone watching me.

How did I get myself into these situations? I moaned as I nudged Repeat into a shuffling walk. Me, who thought reading adventure books was dangerous. Well, I was stuck now, so I knew I'd better just get on with it and hope the fall wouldn't hurt too much. I sighed and clamped my heels down in the stirrups, twisted some mane in one hand, gripped the reins, and chirruped, "Come on, Repeat!"

Nothing happened.

"Louder!" Mr. Richards ordered.

"Come on, Repeat!" I yelled and dug my heels in. He broke into a fast trot.

"He's . . . not . . . can . . . ter . . . ing," I managed to say in between the bumping.

"REPEAT!" Mr. Richards thundered, and suddenly Repeat picked up his feet and everything smoothed out. The corner flashed up, and I held my breath, but Repeat turned on his own. I lost one stirrup and clenched my leg to the saddle, and my reins loosened because I was hanging onto his mane, but I managed to go around twice before Mr. Richards cried, "Stop!"

Repeat stopped before the *p* was out of Mr. Richard's mouth, and I was jolted forward. My jaw smacked his neck, and red-hot pain shot up through my teeth, but at least it was over. I sucked in a breath of air, found my stirrup, gathered up the reins, and proudly walked Repeat back to the center, where even Melissa had a look of admiration on her face.

I smiled at her and sat there basking in happy relief as the others took their turns.

"Do you want to try a different horse next week?" Mr. Richards asked me at the end of the lesson.

I hesitated for a minute, and Mr. Richards lifted his eyebrows and waited while I balanced the certain boredom of Repeat with the uncertain fear of another horse.

"Okay," I said finally. Mr. Richards clapped me on the shoulder.

"Good," he said and walked away.

"That's wonderful!" Mom cried when Melissa and I told her.

"Now you can start riding at home," she announced, unwittingly revealing her master plan.

"Only in your dreams," I said promptly.

Riding school was one thing. Riding any one of our unpredictable trio was another altogether.

# 9

# Outwitting the Tricky Beast OR Survival Beyond the Ring

**Stable horses, sad to say, often have a hard life** despite the care of their owners. They have to put up with all different sorts of riders at any time during the day. Their stalls are usually small, and open pasture time is limited. They develop hard mouths from their reins being jerked by untrained hands, and the boredom of being ridden only in the ring and doing the same routine over and over again causes them to invent irritating little habits, like trying to stop all the time, or catching up to the horse in front and trying to bite him or her.

But the good news is that stable horses also rarely have the energy to attempt anything even remotely dangerous. They just don't have the time or the inclination to dream up the stunts that Really or Sweetheart would pull. Once I learned this, riding school became an easier burden for me. By springtime Melissa and I were both cantering with ease and could walk, trot, post, circle, and do emergency dismounts as well.

I began to think *Is this all there is?* and a new and daring idea entered my mind. *Maybe, just maybe, I could ride Sweetheart in the ring*. But I did not share this radical thought with Melissa. She would have leaped on it like a fly on fresh manure, and I wasn't quite ready yet.

It was a movie, I am embarrassed to admit, that finally convinced me to try. It wasn't *Black Beauty* or *The Black Stallion* or even *National Velvet*. No, it was an old classic that Dad loved: *Lawrence of Arabia*. As a special treat, he allowed Sharon and me to stay up late one school night to watch it. I viewed the whole movie openmouthed (so Sharon said), completely entranced by the sight of men in long, flowing robes flying across the desert sand on purebred Arabian horses. Yes, I became lost in the dream that I had laughed at other girls for having. But the difference was that outside of my house stood my own Arabian mare. So my dream had a solid shape to it.

Of course, I had to gloss over a few facts to keep the dream alive—such as that Sweetheart was sway-backed and her coat was all patchy and gray-brown from rolling in the spring mud. Not to mention that I only had an English saddle, I didn't have a long robe, and Maine in the springtime no-way, no-how resembles a hot Arabian desert, but I wasn't too concerned with particulars. I had a vision: as Lawrence had conquered the desert, I would conquer Sweetheart and race her along the sand down by our beach.

It turned out to be a good thing that I had this dream to sustain me. Melissa announced the next morning on the bus that she was going away for the *whole* summer.

"What?" I cried. "Where to?" My heart absolutely stopped. I couldn't breathe.

"Road trip." Melissa sighed. "We're driving to

Alaska." She tipped her head and imitated her mother's voice, "It'll be a once-in-a-lifetime family vacation." Melissa slumped down in her seat.

"But all our plans? The Clam Festival . . . sleep-overs . . . riding. . . ." My voice trailed off into silence as the horror of it all sank in. I was a little embarrassed to be showing just how upset I was, but I couldn't help it.

"Yeah, riding." Melissa sighed again, and I knew that missing riding would be the worst part for her. She had waited so long and wanted so much to be able to ride outside of the ring. And I had been planning on surprising her with my determination to ride Sweetheart.

So, the summer loomed, suddenly lonely, empty, and fun-less. In school, I surreptitiously studied the girls in my class one by one. There was Susan and her in-town clique, definitely off-limits to me; there was brainy Heidi, who wouldn't come near me; and there were the nose-picking twins, Ethel and Jane. They at least lived on the Island, but they were slobby, weird, and giggly, and I couldn't see us becoming friends.

Then there was Rachel. But after I had been such a jerk in the fall, she had more or less joined in with Susan's gang, and I was sure that by now she had heard what a weirdo I was. Still, maybe it was worth a try. I thought it over for a few days and then screwed up my courage. There is nothing like the prospect of a desperately lonely summer to make you brave.

I carefully worked it so that I was standing beside her in the lunch line.

"Hi, Rachel," I said with a small smile.

"Hi," she said, studying the menu.

"Wasn't that funny when Michael farted during silent reading time? And then went that incredible shade of red?" I plunged ahead.

"Mmm," Rachel said and nodded, her lips not turning upward even a little.

I took a deep breath. "I was wondering . . . do you want to come over sometime and see the horses?" I said this in a rush, adding on the horses for bait.

She at least looked at me; I will give her that. "What, and muck out stalls and clean tack for you? Thanks, but no thanks," she said, and picking up her tray, she walked off without another glance to sit at Susan's table.

I slunk away and slid in beside Melissa at our usual spot. She had no idea what I'd been up to, and pride kept me from telling her.

"It's going to be a long summer." I sighed.

"You can say that again," Melissa agreed glumly.

∩ ∩ ∩

Melissa's family was so gung ho about going on this vacation that they left one week before school let out. (Now, why couldn't my parents ever do that?) On Monday, I dragged myself around to classes, skipped lunch, and read a book in the library to avoid the awfulness of having to eat alone. But after lunch came science, and I was dreading this class because we worked in teams, and Melissa was always my partner. Mr. Perkins never allowed us to work alone, and sure enough, when he noticed Melissa's empty seat, he boomed out, "Sophie, you can work with Heidi and Rachel!"

I groaned inwardly as I gathered up my things. I would have rather worked with Susan than Rachel at this point, but there was no use arguing. I picked up my stool and moved to their table. Heidi nervously tried to pick up her mountain of messy notebooks and jam-spotted papers. Rachel ignored me and listened to Mr. Perkins as he explained how we would search for plastic skeletons in a sand-filled box. We were supposed to pretend to be archaeologists on a dig—Mr. Perkins's idea of end-of-the-year "science fun."

For a while all three of us worked in silence, while everyone else around us laughed, showed off the bones they'd discovered, and cracked ghoulish jokes.

"Now, we have to find a tibia in the eighth sector," Heidi read from the instruction sheet, while Rachel and I searched through the sand with toothbrushes. Heidi adjusted her glasses yet again. "And then we should find a—"

"Hey! I found something," Rachel cried. "It's . . . It's . . . a piece of candy!" she said, holding up a chocolate wrapped in red foil.

"You did?" I said, perking up for the first time that day.

"That's not on the instruction sheet," Heidi said in a worried tone.

"Let's look for more!" Rachel said, and the hunt was on. We abandoned the toothbrushes and sifted sand with our fingers.

"Guys, stop!" Heidi pleaded desperately, but we ignored her.

"This archaeology stuff is fun," Rachel declared.

"It's like looking for buried treasure," I agreed, and together we flung aside two hands, a leg, and a skull.

Heidi threw down her notebook and stomped off to find Mr. Perkins.

"I guess it was just a mistake," I said when we had searched through the whole box and didn't find any more candy.

"You want to split this?" Rachel offered.

"Sure," I said, glad that we were at least speaking to each other.

We were munching it down when Heidi returned with Mr. Perkins.

"A piece of ancient candy, eh?" he asked, rubbing his hands together. "Do you girls see what the prospect of gold can do to the science of archaeology?" He looked pointedly at the jumbled pile of bones heaped in one corner of the box. "You have just learned how greed has ruined so many fine archaeological sites," he explained.

"Oh," Rachel and I said, feeling a little sheepish.

"What do we do now?" Heidi asked. Anything outside of the normal routine made her uneasy.

"Eat some candy, Heidi," Mr. Perkins said as he handed her a piece from his pocket. "And remember that this was the point of today's lesson."

All around us were cries of "Hey! Candy!" and arguments over who would get to eat it. Mr. Perkins beamed at the success of his experiment and strode off to observe the results of the other teams. Heidi sniffed disgustedly and buried herself in a book, and Rachel asked me if I wanted to come over sometime and go swimming. Among all the racket of the candy hunting, I wasn't sure if I had heard her right.

"If it's sunny, we'll go swimming in my pool. It's heated," she added.

"You have a swimming pool?" I said, lighting up. "Wow."

"Yes, lots of people like to come over because I have one. So I make them vacuum it and then empty the catch basket, which usually has gross things in it like bugs and worms and sometimes even a dead mouse," Rachel said, sorting idly through the bones. "And sometimes I tell them the story of how we once added too much chlorine, and my skin turned all red and itchy for days," she continued.

"Oh," I said, not quite sure how to answer.

"And then they usually don't want to come over to swim anymore," she concluded with a small shrug.

She looked at me, and I looked at her, and then I realized she was getting me back—and I couldn't help it, I laughed. And when Rachel laughed with me, the spring sunshine suddenly seemed brighter and the sky bluer.

Maybe, just maybe, it was going to be an okay summer after all.

∩ ∩ ∩

Within a week of riding lessons ending and school letting out, I had mastered riding Sweetheart-in-the-Ring. But that was the easy part, and now came the moment of truth. I had to attempt Sweetheart-out-of-the-Ring, an entirely different creature. And, to add to the problem, she hadn't been ridden a lot that spring, since my sister had been preoccupied with the mirror, her friends, and her new job as an Island camp counselor.

To make matters worse, Rachel was supposed to come over on Saturday to see the horses. The week before I'd gone swimming in her pool, and we'd had such a good time that, for the first time in my life, I actually wanted to take someone riding. But first I had to dispel the myth (well, okay, it was true) that I was afraid of my own horses, and this meant daring to ride Sweetheart-out-of-the-Ring before Rachel's visit.

All the months of riding lessons and a week of riding Sweetheart-in-the-Ring, doing everything from jumping buckets to jumping off without any problems, didn't stop the old heart-hammering fear from rising up in my throat when Mom opened that gate.

But I knew I had to do it.

"Ride down across the Narrows, up the hill, and turn around at the beginning of the woods," she instructed firmly.

I nodded, too scared, as usual, to talk.

"And watch for the tree trick," Mom said knowingly.

I walked Sweetheart through the gate, and the minute we were past it, she began to cough pitifully. I dug in my heels, and she stopped midcough and began to limp. I reached down and whacked her lightly on the shoulder. She snorted, picked up her feet, and we were off. Round one had ended, and I was the victor. But the fight, as we were both well aware, was far from over.

Dad was stationed on Gramp's lawn to watch, and he waved encouragement from his chair. Down across the Narrows I could see Gramp's truck parked under "Sweetheart's Tree" on the knoll. Good old Gramp. Now Sweetheart wouldn't be able to dash under the tree and knock me off. I walked Sweetheart across the Narrows and up the hill, where I waved at Gramp. He tooted from the cab of the truck.

I came to the woods. I took a deep breath, dug my heels down, tightened the reins, and swung Sweetheart around for home. Immediately her head and tail shot up, and her feet lifted into a high-stepping, bum-pounding prance. Her age drained away from her, and she was a filly again as she jerked her head up and down and set her mane flapping. And it occurred to me that perhaps she, too, was dreaming of deserts.

She gave a little buck and shied sideways as she started down the hill. I lost both my stirrups and had to use one hand to grab her mane. Sweetheart, as always, sensed her opportunity and lurched into a canter while swerving sideways. She darted around Gramp's truck and under the branch on the other side of the tree. I ducked but felt the bark brush my hair.

Sweetheart raced across the Narrows with me clinging to her back like a starfish. Riding lessons had at least given me strong legs and a good grip. We flew by Dad and tore down the road toward the barn. Sweetheart raced up the drive and then slid to a halt. Gravel flew everywhere as I bounced up onto her neck and fell back again.

Mom came running up and grabbed the reins. "Are you all right?" she asked.

I sat up slowly. I felt dizzy and a little sick. I gulped for air.

"I stayed on," I said incredulously.

"What?" Mom said.

I know what she had been expecting. She had thought I would cry. I thought I would cry, too, but I didn't. I smiled and then I laughed and slid off. "Tomorrow, I'll try it again," I announced with a pat to Sweetheart's heaving chest.

And the next day I did ride her again—only this time I held on to the reins tighter, ducked when I had to, and managed to keep Sweetheart to a fast prance all the way home. By the time we arrived at the barn, my hands and my rear end were cramped and numb, but I had made it home still on her back and even somewhat in control. Sweetheart fixed me with a cool look of assessment and almost—but maybe I only imagined it—respect. And later, when I was running a long, hot bath for myself, I looked out the bathroom window and noticed that the three horses were huddled together in what looked like a conference on the paddock manure pile.

They all seemed wary when I approached on Wednesday, a new spring in my step. I rode all the way around the Point that day, and when we turned for home, Sweetheart pranced, but there was no bucking or shying or trips to "the tree."

On Thursday, I gathered up my courage, cried "Hat-tut-tut," which was Lawrence of Arabia's wild camel cry, and we thundered across the Narrows, up the hill, and into the trees. There I reined her in, and Sweetheart stopped and tossed her head, her bit jingling. She had enjoyed the canter, I realized, and what's more, so had I. (She also enjoyed the prance on the way home, however, which I did not.)

On Friday we cantered across the beach. It was

slower because the sand was heavy and wet. Sweetheart's sides heaved as we walked up the hill—but we had done it. I had at last ridden an Arabian across the sands. I stopped to pat Sweetheart's neck, knowing that I was at last ready to show Rachel that I could handle my horses.

*Eat dirt, Lawrence of Arabia!* I thought with satisfaction.

# 10

# Try, Try Again OR Learning to Get Back On

**Rachel came on Saturday, as arranged. Before she** arrived, I had a long chat with Sweetheart, which included lots of sugar, and then I saddled her. Sweetheart was dozing in the shade of the pine tree at the corner of the paddock when Rachel's mom dropped her off.

"Here she is," I said after we said hello to each other. Rachel walked to the fence and timidly patted her neck. "Where are the others?" she asked.

"Out there," I said, pointing to where the Giant and the Midget watched from the pasture. They hated to be banished from the action, but I wasn't taking any chances.

I opened the gate. "Come on in. Do you want to ride first?" I offered, quite proud of myself.

"Well . . . I . . . maybe I'll just watch," Rachel said quickly.

I recognized that tone of hesitation.

"Sweetheart's gentle as a lamb in the ring," I said reassuringly. "But we don't have to ride," I added hastily, knowing how often I had wished someone would say that to me.

"No, I want to," Rachel said. She reached out to

stroke Sweetheart's neck. "But I've never been on a horse before," she admitted.

I showed Rachel how to scratch Sweetheart's neck so that she arched it in pleasure and tickle Sweetheart's nose until she laughed and bared her teeth. And then I showed Rachel how to open her hand flat and feed Sweetheart sugar cubes.

"I know I shouldn't be scared," Rachel said. "I mean, what could happen?"

I opened my mouth to tell her but then stopped myself.

Later, I wished I had warned her since, unfortunately, she was about to find out—along with Dad. He and Gramp were unloading building supplies for the new dock from the truck and carrying them to the spare stall in the barn.

I unhooked Sweetheart and showed Rachel how to get on. I rode around the paddock trying to demonstrate how to use double reins to steer. But it was hard for Rachel to see from the ground.

"Let's ride double. It'll be easier for me to show you," I suggested. It seemed like a fine idea at the time.

Rachel agreed, so I had her climb up on the fence, and then I helped her onto Sweetheart's back. She sat behind the saddle and hung on to my waist. Sweetheart groaned in protest but otherwise put up with this nonsense.

I steered around the paddock carefully and slowly. I didn't tell Rachel that I had never ridden double before. Melissa would kill me if she ever found out, as she had been suggesting it for ages. I steered away from the gate to the pasture, where the other two horses were watching our every move with interest.

I didn't want Rachel's leg to get anywhere near Really's sharp teeth.

Rachel was laughing and chatting, and I was happy, too. I'd even started to consider the idea that riding horses *was* a good way to make friends after all—when Gramp lost his grip on a heavy sheet of plywood. Unfortunately, we were right down at his end at the time, and when it landed with a loud bang, Sweetheart reared up in surprise. She came down and ran zigzag at breakneck speed across the ring. Rachel flew off immediately into the dirt, but I hung on until Sweetheart came to a jarring stop by the pasture gate. Then I vaulted off across her neck, flew headfirst over the fence, and slammed straight into Fancy's massive stomach. There was a lot of neighing (from the horses), and screaming (from me), and thundering hooves, and then silence.

Had I died? Was I paralyzed? Would I ever walk again? I lay there in the tall grass of the paddock, looking up at the blue sky, too stunned to move. Then the light was blocked and Gramp was there, leaning over and talking to me.

"Golly, Sophie, I'm *wicked* sorry," he said as he helped me to sit up. He got out his handkerchief and held it to my head. When he pulled it away, I saw blood.

Suddenly I felt sick to my stomach. "How bad is it? Do I have to go to the hospital?" I managed to whisper.

"Just a scratch," Gramp said, patting my arm. "Maybe a stitch or two."

*Stitches!* I moaned and lay back down in the grass. Gramp wisely went and got Dad, who had been helping Rachel.

"Sit up," Dad ordered. He inspected the damage closely. "I want Mom," I whimpered, knowing full well she was away at an art show.

"Now, Sophie, it's only a small cut. We can fix it up with a butterfly bandage. You need to take care of your friend," he added as he helped me to my feet.

I swung around to peer at Rachel, huddled miserably underneath the pine tree, and the pain of my injury was instantly replaced by the deeper ache of knowing that after this episode, she would never, ever be my friend. I could see Susan laughing, and Heidi nodding her head in sympathy. My summer was doomed.

I sat down next to Rachel while Dad went to get the bacterial spray and a bandage. She wouldn't look at me, but at least she wasn't bleeding. She had stopped crying and shaking, but we both sat silently as Gramp fed us lemonade and cookies.

"Sugar's the best thing for shock," Gramp offered. "When I caught my arm in the outhaul and nearly tore it off—"

"Go catch the horse," Dad said, arriving back on the scene and cutting him off before he could share any more gruesome details. Gramp shrugged and wandered off.

Dad finished patching me up, and I ran my fingers over my forehead, touching the bandage and the growing bump beneath it. He then helped us both up and led us over to the corner of the paddock.

"Now, girls," he said gently, "it's a hard thing to do, but you have to get back on the horse. Otherwise, you'll never have the courage to do it again."

*Right now?* I snuck a glance at Rachel. She was

staring at Dad like he'd just suggested we jump off the bridge to the Island (on the rocky side).

"No way!" I said immediately.

Dad ignored me and pointed to Sweetheart, who was now standing calmly beside Gramp. "She's a gentle horse. She was just scared by the noise." And she did appear to be sorry. Her head hung down, her reins drooped around her neck, and she wouldn't look at us.

Dad helped us over the fence. Rachel hesitated, but he had her up and over by the time she opened her mouth to say no.

"Pet her," Dad ordered.

I stretched out one arm as far as it would go and gave Sweetheart's neck a quick touch. Rachel copied me.

"Okay, now Sophie, you first. I'll help you, and Gramp will hold the reins. It'll be fine," Dad tried to reassure me.

But that was farther than I intended to go. I planted my feet into the ground and folded my arms across my chest. Rachel looked from me to Dad and back again, unsure what to do.

"Sophie!" Dad hissed, but I refused to budge.

We were heading toward a standoff when Gramp cut in. "Maybe you should ride her first, Ed," he suggested.

Things became very quiet at that point. Dad's mouth opened, but he said nothing for a long moment, and I realized then that I had never actually seen my father *on* a horse before.

"I'm too heavy for her swayback," Dad said finally, shaking his head.

"Oh, I'm sure once around won't kill the old girl," Gramp said with a fond pat to Sweetheart's neck.

Sweetheart responded by rubbing her head along his arm, leaving a trail of saliva and white hair all over Gramp's shirt. It was her way of showing affection.

Dad's eyes narrowed to slits, and he flashed Gramp a look that clearly said *I'll get you later.* He stomped around to Sweetheart's left side and hoisted himself up and into the saddle. Sweetheart snorted loudly in protest and tossed up her head. Dad froze and suddenly turned a very interesting shade of pale green.

"Want me to lead you?" Gramp offered kindly.

Dad ignored him and pulled Sweetheart's head around. He clucked to her and started off. I held my breath while they plodded down the paddock, watched closely by humans on one side and horses on the other (they had cautiously returned to their position at the gate).

But nothing happened, and Gramp turned to Rachel and me. "Every year we used to go up to Union to visit my cousins who ran a dairy farm. One time, when Ed was oh, about ten, they were riding the cows in to be milked when something happened. I'm not sure what, maybe a bee stung the cow, but, anyway, your father's cow went berserk! Took off running and bucked your father off into a raspberry patch. We fished him out and cleaned up the scratches, and he was fine, but he absolutely refused to ride any animal after that. Gave up on his cowboy dream and took up fishing."

Gramp sighed and leaned back against the fence. "Yup, stubborn as a mule, just like someone else I know," he said with a sly glance in my direction.

I was relieved to see Rachel smile, though I didn't

care too much for the comment.

Dad pulled in to the corner and stopped. He swung a leg around in front and slid off. He gave Gramp a look of cool satisfaction before offering the reins to me.

My stomach was not feeling too good, but I knew when I was cornered. I had to get on or else I'd never live it down with any of them. Still, my hands shook as I took the reins from Dad, and I was too wobbly to get on without help. I rode around once, very slowly, gripping the reins so tightly that Sweetheart jerked her head up and down in protest. My heart stopped racing, and I took a few deep breaths as I turned and rode around the other way.

Now it was Rachel's turn. She still didn't utter a word, but she allowed Dad to help her on, and then I led her around the ring holding the bridle tightly. Dad gave me a thumbs-up sign, and then he and Gramp retreated to drink coffee under the oak tree behind the barn. After two more times around, I unsaddled Sweetheart, and we brushed her and sent her out to roll in the field.

Then we walked down to the beach to go wading.

"Well," Rachel said, speaking at last, "that's a riding lesson I'll never forget." I looked over at her and saw that she was at last a normal color and smiling. A great wave of relief flooded over me and, for a moment, I forgot my throbbing head and bruised elbow.

"Me, either," I agreed.

We spent the rest of the day at the beach laughing and talking and daring each other to wade deeper in the still freezing-cold water.

When Rachel left, I went to the barn to clean the stalls. It had been a good day after all, I decided. Rachel wasn't Melissa, but she was fun in her own way and not afraid to admit the truth about things. She had even confessed that she didn't like Susan, who only came over to use her pool, and that she had been afraid of the water until she was eight. She was a really brave person, I decided as I rolled the wheelbarrow out onto the chip dump. Best of all, she hadn't wanted to spend all day with the horses, I thought, as I filled the water and grain buckets.

I walked out to the field, where the three horses stood clustered by the gate, their heads poking through or hanging above, waiting for the food they knew was in their stalls. I unlatched the gate, thinking, no, it wasn't cowardly to have enough sense to be afraid of something. You just have to keep trying in your own way and time, and eventually—even with horses—you can win.

I was so busy thinking all this that I stood there distracted. Fancy, impatient for dinner, shoved her mighty body against the gate. It swung open and caught me square in the chest, knocking me down on the ground for the second time that day. Fancy thundered past me, hell-bent for the barn. I caught a flash of white underbelly as Sweetheart leaped nimbly over me, and then Really dashed by, stopping only to nip me on the arm before she followed the others.

I heard them pounding up the ramp to their stalls, and then all was silent except for the chomping of grain. I sat up, rubbed at the teeth marks on my arm, and shook my head.

I was wrong. There are some things that just never change no matter what you do.

# 11

# The Battle with Debbie OR Soaring the Steel Steed

**Rachel and I were lazing on the lawn one morning** in July, thinking it was way too hot to do anything, when we heard a diesel truck rumble into the barn driveway. I was just working up the energy to go see who it could be when the sun was blocked by three figures. My heart began to gallop, and I shivered in the heat as Rachel and I scrambled to our feet.

"What are *you* doing here?" I asked the Carpwells.

Seeing my horrified expression, Debbie's mouth curved up in a thin line that reminded me of the Grinch. She could sniff fear a mile off. She turned to Rachel, who smiled back at her, unaware of the danger she was now in.

"Had to deliver a year-old beef steer to the Bowden farm," Judd informed us.

"What happened to your hand?" Rachel asked. I looked at Judd, and sure enough, half of his right hand and three of his fingers were wrapped in grungy gauze. Judd scowled and didn't answer.

"He lost a bet and had to jump down the hay chute from the upper loft," Debbie explained with a smirk. "He landed on a pitchfork."

Rachel sucked in her breath. "Did . . . did it go

through your hand?" she asked.

Judd laughed, not bothered at all by the gross image. "Nah, just crushed it when the rest of me landed on top."

"Where's Sharon?" Lori interrupted.

"Up-island with friends," I said, wishing I was there, too. If I had known the Carpwells were dropping by, Rachel and I would have been far, far away.

"Too bad she's going to miss it." Lori sighed.

I was afraid to ask but couldn't resist. "Miss what?"

Debbie led the way, and we all followed, even Rachel, who I think was beginning to understand it would be unwise not to.

"We traded the heifer that we raised," Debbie said, unlatching the back gate of the horse trailer they towed.

"*I* raised him!" Judd interjected.

"We!" Debbie snapped back as she lowered the gate.

"I!" Judd insisted.

"We!"

"I!"

This was heading for a fistfight. I was about to shove Rachel to safety when Debbie and Judd suddenly stopped arguing—as Lori backed a gleaming black, blue, and chrome four-wheeler out of the trailer.

Wow. Dad called them death machines and had forbidden Sharon and me to even think of riding one. I quickly looked at my house, but there was no movement.

"Start it up," Debbie ordered.

To my credit, I did manage a "no!" but my puny protest was drowned out by the throaty roar of the four-stroke engine. The horses, out grazing in the field, immediately lifted up their heads, surveyed the scene, and cantered off to the farthest corner, where they huddled together in a pack. I wished I could do the same. But I didn't dare to leave. Plus, there was a certain horrifying fascination with seeing what was going to happen. I glanced again at the quiet house.

Debbie hopped on in her shorts and sandals.

"She has no helmet," Rachel said into my ear.

"Don't say anything!" I hissed. Rachel gave me a startled look but smartly kept quiet. We moved into the shade of the pine tree while Lori opened the gate to the field. Debbie shifted into first and zoomed off through the high grass, her kinky blonde hair flying all around her head. She flew down toward the end, causing the horses to jump and gallop away to the other corner. Debbie wheeled around, came back, and Judd jumped on behind her. He held onto her waist with one hand, the other bandaged one held high as they jounced over tractor ruts. Lori was next, and her ride was even faster, since Debbie was getting the hang of steering and changing gears. She roared back up, and as Lori stepped off, Debbie pointed a finger at Rachel.

Rachel's mouth opened but no sound came out, at least not one that could be heard above the idling engine. Finally, Rachel took a step forward—and something in me snapped. I would not, could not, let the friend that I'd worked so hard to gain be scared to death by the wicked Debbie Carpwell.

"No!" I cried, and all eyes swung toward me in complete surprise. "It's my turn!" I rushed forward and hopped on behind Debbie before I lost my nerve.

Debbie's eyes narrowed at this twist of her command.

"Hang on!" she ordered, but I didn't need to be told. I gripped the leather belt on her hips so tightly, my knuckles turned white. I tried not to think about my helmet-less head cracking like an egg if I fell off.

Debbie shifted into first gear, and we shot off down the field. First she zigzagged, then she swerved, and, finally, she stopped short. But I was now an experienced rider and discovered, both to her surprise and mine, that I couldn't be easily shaken off. Debbie rolled one green eye back toward me, and I could see her sizing up my newfound courage. Which was sheer bluff because I was actually so scared that I was breathing in gulps and needed to pee like a racehorse.

Debbie pressed down on the thumb throttle, and we picked up speed again. We arced in a wide loop around the now-sweating horses and headed up toward the barn. Debbie swung left just before it, and—too late to jump off—I realized what she intended to do. Directly ahead of us lay our manure pile. It hadn't been spread out since early spring and was now a hill of chips and poop at least eight feet high.

"Stop!" I screeched—all courage forgotten. I wanted to live! But it was too late. We fishtailed our way up the mound and then shot out over the top, airborne for—one one-thousand, two one-thousand, three one-thousand—seconds. Then the four-wheeler slammed back down onto the hill, Debbie slammed into the handlebars, and I slammed into Debbie.

We rolled to a stop. Judd ran over and cut the engine as I fell off, my legs shaking too badly to stand.

Debbie sat up and clutched her nose. Blood

poured through her fingers. Judd whipped off his T-shirt and gave it to her. She wadded it up under her nose and turned toward me.

"You knocked me into the handlebars!" she hollered from underneath the cloth.

"You shouldn't have jumped the manure pile!" I yelled back, too shaken by the ride and the blood to be scared of her.

"Yeah—but you should have seen it! You guys cleared three feet of air," Judd said, awed by our feat.

"Really?" Debbie took the cloth away and grinned, her teeth streaked a gruesome pink from the blood. Lori leaned forward and shoved the cloth back in place despite Debbie's protest.

"Heck—yeah! I want to try it next," Judd declared.

"You can't," Lori pointed out. "You only have one hand."

"No problem," Judd said waving his bandaged fist. "Someone can ride behind me and press the accelerator."

I stopped breathing, and even Lori looked a little unsure about this plan. Fortunately, we were spared from this deadly experiment by the appearance of Dad and an angry Mr. Carpwell.

"Hey!" he shouted. "Get that thing back in the van. You know you're not allowed to ride without a helmet!"

"We were just going slowly around the paddock. Sophie wanted a ride before we left," Debbie lied smoothly, thrusting the bloody T-shirt behind her back and quickly wiping her now-dried-up nose.

"I did not!" I protested. Rachel quickly elbowed me. She had already sized up Debbie and figured I'd done enough for one day. But I was beyond reason—

and intent on running my mouth.

"Did too!" Debbie snarled, stepping closer to me.

"Did not!" I placed my hands on my hips.

"Get in the truck!" Mr. Carpwell ordered. "And put on a shirt!" he said to Judd, who had returned from loading the four-wheeler.

Now we were in trouble. If Mr. Carpwell saw Judd's bloody T-shirt, we would all have some explaining to do. There was an awkward pause, and then I spoke again.

"Your shirt's in the barn, Judd," I said and led him inside to the rag box. Fortunately, there was one of Dad's old T-shirts that wasn't too grungy and only had one hole in the back. Judd slipped it on, and all three Carpwell kids piled into the king-cab truck before Mr. Carpwell noticed anything.

Debbie caught my eye and gave a small wave as they pulled out. I waved back, hoping her gesture meant that she knew I couldn't be pushed around anymore.

"Interesting people," Rachel remarked when the truck had disappeared from sight. But before I could say "You mean *insane*!" Dad turned to me.

"I don't want you anywhere near one of those things ever again—with or without a helmet!" he ordered, and then stalked off to the fish shack.

He didn't have to worry. I looked over at the sweaty horses, who had crept back up to the gate, and they looked at me. For once, I knew we were in agreement. Riding for us would not involve wheels!

# 12

# The Wild West Horse OR Bigger Is Not Always Better

**By midsummer, Sweetheart and I had ridden all** over the Island, on every trail, road, beach, and driveway. She no longer pranced on the way home, generally being too tired. And now and again, I could even let the reins droop.

Sweetheart was a fairly good sport, but she was no trail horse. She hated to get her feet wet; she shied at anything that moved in the brush; and cars, people, bicycles, and dogs scared her. When she was nervous, she would roll her eyes, arch her neck and tail, and prance away sideways.

People were impressed by this performance, as they were meant to be. Jumpy she might be, but Sweetheart was also vain and loved nothing better than a slightly terrified audience. This trait made conversations difficult, though, as I was jolted up and down like a jackhammer when she did it. Other kids could ride their bikes to the Island center and flop them down on the grass around the old water pump, but I could only wave and say a quick hi before Sweetheart would dance away.

Sometimes this was glamorous and fun. Other times I wondered why my mother couldn't have been at least a little bit normal and bought us bikes like everyone else. She insisted that because we had horses, we didn't need bikes. And there was no use asking Dad. He was still waiting to buy a new boat.

When Melissa finally returned in August, she was thrilled about my newly developed riding bravery, and we took turns cantering Sweetheart across the Narrows and around the Point. Once Melissa had established that she, too, could hold the reins, duck under tree branches, and stay on, Sweetheart accepted defeat gracefully and did as we asked—most of the time.

There was one time when Melissa forgot the lesson to never canter a horse home. Sweetheart had gathered speed, and she was running at a full gallop by the time she reached the barn. She screeched to a halt, and Mom and I arrived just in time to see Melissa sail over her head and land in a heap on the gravel. I scolded Sweetheart while Melissa picked the gravel out of her elbows.

But other than that accident—which would have really upset me but which, of course, Melissa barely noticed—we had great fun. It was not, however, quite the same as riding together. One of us was always waiting for the other, and my mother forbid riding double because of Sweetheart's swayback and neck goiter (and because of what had happened to Rachel—but I decided not to mention this to Melissa).

"Sophie, we've just got to learn to ride Fancy," Melissa said finally. We were sitting on the paddock fence looking out at the three amigas, all grazing together in a line, largest to smallest. There was a definite social order among the three. Fancy was undisputedly the captain, Sweetheart was the first mate, and Really the common sailor—but Sweetheart and Really bickered a lot because each wanted to be Fancy's favorite. Fancy tried to be fair to each, but she seesawed back and forth between Sweetheart's tricky ways and Really's meanness.

This triangle of intrigue made me think of Rachel, and I sighed. After what had turned out to be a fun summer, I had simply assumed that Melissa and Rachel and I would all be friends. I would, I thought happily, for the first time be part of a gang. But that was not the way things were working out.

"Rachel! You hung out with *her* all summer?" Melissa scoffed when I had first told her. "She's one of Susan's gang."

"No, really, Melissa—she's not. She's fun and nice. And she has a heated swimming pool," I added.

Melissa snorted in disgust, and I knew I'd said the wrong thing.

Rachel wasn't any better. "Don't you think Melissa's just, you know, a little bit *strange*?" she asked.

"Well, she is outspoken, but she's really brave," I said, defending Melissa. "She's the only person who has ever ridden Really for more than three minutes. She lasted through eight attempts to buck, kick, and roll her," I informed Rachel proudly.

Rachel raised her eyebrows at me. "It might be brave, but it doesn't show a lot of sense," she said logically.

So, I couldn't explain to Rachel why I liked Melissa, and I couldn't explain to Melissa why I liked Rachel. And, as school loomed closer, I knew I had a problem. I tried to juggle both friendships. With Rachel I went swimming and shopping and gossiped. With Melissa I went riding and exploring and had adventures. But it was an uneasy truce. And so, when Melissa suggested riding Fancy, I gave in to keep the peace.

"But only in the ring," I added.

"Sure," Melissa said as she hopped off the fence and walked toward the gate. "For now," she tossed over her shoulder.

I sighed for about the millionth time since I'd known her, and followed.

∩ ∩ ∩

Riding Fancy presented problems that were nothing like the problems with riding Sweetheart, or even Really. You didn't have to outsmart Fancy, as she was generally easygoing and sweet-tempered. But her very size made riding Fancy potentially dangerous. Even Mom recognized this fact and told Dad to keep an eye on us as he fixed traps outside the barn.

Our first difficulty was that Fancy never allowed anyone to tie her up so we had to saddle her in her stall. And she was so tall that I had to overturn a water bucket in order to reach her back. We also discovered that a Western saddle, though beautiful with its tooled leather and big stirrups, is heavy. I could barely lift it, much less hoist it up onto Fancy's back. And when I did finally manage to heave it upward, she would shift away from me at the last minute.

After five failed attempts in which both the saddle and I landed in the wood chips, I lurched to the stall door, dumped the saddle on it, and collapsed outside, sweat rolling down my face. Fancy swung her head over the door and looked down at Melissa and me with a perplexed expression on her face, not understanding why we had stopped.

"You girls okay in there?" Dad hollered.

"Yes, Mr. Groves," Melissa answered, because I was still too winded.

When I finally caught my breath, Melissa and I hatched a new plan, and we went back in the stall together. While I stood on the bucket and lifted the saddle, Melissa stationed herself on Fancy's other side, ready to shove her back my way should she move.

"Ready?" I asked.

"Ready," Melissa answered.

I raised the saddle, promptly lost my balance, and fell into Fancy's side, with the pommel of the saddle hitting her directly in the stomach. Fancy snorted in surprise and swung away from me. Again I fell down into the shavings with the saddle.

"Melissa?" I called out, but there was no answer.

I jumped up and hit Fancy on the rear. "Move!" I hollered, and she stepped away from the wall, revealing a very smooshed and white Melissa.

"Ahhh." Melissa wheezed and slid to the floor. I helped her outside and then fetched the saddle.

*"Geez Louise!"* she said as she gasped for breath. "That horse could kill someone and not even know it."

"Yup; I tried to tell you, Melissa—sweet but dumb," I agreed.

But I knew better than to think that event would change Melissa's mind about riding Fancy. Sure enough, it didn't. This time I stood against one wall with the saddle, and Melissa pushed Fancy toward me. As soon as she got close, I lifted the saddle up and slid it onto her back.

It took another fifteen minutes to figure out the

girth. Western saddles are not only heavier but more complicated. The girth, usually all leather, crosses behind the forelegs, goes up through a ring, down through a second ring, and up to the first ring again. And it takes practice to know how to tighten it.

"I guess it's okay," Melissa said as we studied the picture in the book on Western riding that we'd borrowed from the library. Fancy stood patiently, chewing some hay.

"Looks right," I agreed.

The bridle was easier. Unlike Sweetheart, Fancy needed only a small snaffle bit, and Western bridles have only one rein on each side. But I was very careful as I raised my arm over Fancy's eyes—because I knew for certain that if I spooked Fancy, parts of my body would definitely become broken.

At last we were ready. Melissa opened the gate to the paddock, and I opened the stall door. I would like to say that I led Fancy to the ring, but in truth she led me, and I stumbled along, trying to keep up.

Luckily for me, Fancy was so well trained that she stopped the minute we reached the paddock. Now loomed the problem of actually trying to get on her. At first, I climbed to the top board of the fence, and Melissa tried to lead her over to me. But every time we got close to the fence, Fancy would swing away.

"She doesn't like being so close to the fence," Melissa said, rubbing her shoulder, which was sore from Fancy almost jerking it out of its socket each time she shied away.

"How about a bucket?" I suggested. So Melissa fed her an apple while I gently set down an overturned bucket beside her. I grasped the pommel of the saddle with one hand, lifted my foot up, and barely managed to catch the stirrup with my toes. I heaved upward as Fancy shifted away, but I was able to haul myself almost onto the saddle. My arms clutched desperately at the pommel, and I dropped the stirrup, leaving my feet dangling uselessly in the air.

"Help!" I cried, and suddenly I felt Melissa shove my legs upward with all her might. I shot over the saddle and crashed to the ground on the other side.

Melissa rushed around and helped me stand.

"Sorry," she said.

"Did you have to push so hard?" I complained as I felt my bruised bum.

The second try was better. Fancy still shied away, but I grasped the pommel with both hands, and after a short struggle, hauled myself up. I swung my right leg over the saddle, but the world tilted and suddenly I was sliding sideways. Fancy snorted as I slipped down between her legs and landed in a heap. She shifted her feet in surprise, and I shot out from underneath her legs, crawling as fast as I could to safety.

I dusted myself off while Melissa soothed the horse. Fancy hadn't spooked, but she looked mighty uncomfortable with the saddle hanging down under her stomach. I held Fancy's reins while Melissa carefully undid the loosened girth and the saddle dropped into the dirt. Then she dragged it out and hoisted it up on the fence.

Dad came over to check on our progress, and we all studied the picture in the book again. We led Fancy back inside and repeated the saddling routine, only this time Dad heaved on the girth each time we slipped it through a ring. Fancy shook her massive head at us, but she didn't resist our amateur attempts. When we led her back to the paddock, I hung off the pommel with all my weight, and it remained tight. Melissa patted Fancy and then helped shove me, until at last I sat upright in the saddle.

Immediately the old familiar fear strangled my throat. Breakfast rose up from my stomach, and I choked it back down. I was miles off the ground and Melissa looked far, far away.

"Well?" Melissa prompted.

"It's really high," I managed to squeak out.

I took a deep breath and screwed up enough courage to turn and walk Fancy around the paddock. Fancy did everything I asked, and the saddle stayed in place. I began to breathe again. After a few more minutes, I trotted. It took some time getting used to holding the reins in one hand. Instead of pulling on the rein to turn right, I simply moved my hand to the right, which made the left rein lay across her neck and thus told her to swing to the right. To help give her the correct signal, I also pressed my left leg against her side.

"Nothing to it," I called out to Melissa and then gave her a turn.

We spent the next two weekends figuring out Fancy's good points: She was sweet and tame and followed commands well. She had been taught to stay with her rider, so you could dismount and walk anywhere and she would follow after you like a patient dog. She also had a great slow jog to which you could just sit and bounce a little.

She also, sad to say, had her bad points: She was so good at following commands that she would walk straight off the dock if you asked her to, she always shied away when you tried to mount her, and she never seemed to understand how strong she was. She was constantly squishing, stepping on, or shoving one of us and always looked hurt when we hollered at her.

But overall, we concluded, she was a "good horse," despite her size. And it wasn't until the end of our second week of riding her that we discovered her one major flaw: She had the worst, most stiff-legged, bone-jarring, tooth-loosening canter I had ever experienced. Lulled into complacency by Sweetheart's rolling gait, I hadn't even thought about it. I had just assumed Fancy would be as smooth as Sweetheart and the other stable horses I had ridden.

But when I finally drummed up the courage to canter her (me first, on Mom's orders), I immediately lost both stirrups, dropped the reins, and became instantly grateful that there is a pommel on a Western saddle—as I had to cling to it to keep from falling off.

"Wh . . . oo . . . aa . . . oo . . . ahhh!" I ordered. Fancy halted immediately, with one final bum-bruising jolt.

"What's wrong?" Melissa cried, running up as I slid stiffly to the ground.

"Nothing," I managed to say. "Your turn." I smiled and helped her on.

Melissa circled the paddock twice—but neither one of us felt very good that night. The problem, to be fair to Fancy, was not only her canter, but also that a Western saddle does not have the padding of an English one. We realized this as we hobbled down the hallway in school the next day, trying not to wince as we sat down. We swore ourselves to absolute secrecy on the subject as the jokes would have been endless if any of the boys had found out why we were limping.

On the bus home, we discussed the problem.

"We could pad the saddle," Melissa suggested.

"Yeah, and fall off with it when it slips," I pointed out.

In the end, we resorted to padding our jodhpurs with folded pairs of old flannel pajamas. We looked ridiculous waddling out to the ring, and my sister laughed herself silly when she saw us. But it did help a little.

"She might be smoother when she's cantering in a straight line—outside of the paddock," Melissa suggested.

"Maybe," I said, knowing Melissa would say almost anything to get me to try it.

But that would be the most dangerous thing I had ever attempted. Fancy was as large as an elephant, and a flying fall from her . . . well, I shuddered to imagine it. So, I politely ignored Melissa's suggestion. And I would have gone on ignoring her—except that she had help arrive, in the form of Ben St. Cyr, the blacksmith.

# 13

# A Visit from the Blacksmith OR How I Lost My Common Sense

**Every spring Ben St. Cyr came to shoe the horses,** and every fall he came to remove the shoes for the winter. We all loved to watch him work, not only because it was interesting, but because he was such a jolly guy and a great storyteller. He'd been around hundreds of horses and always had a new story to tell, sometimes gruesome, sometimes funny. Dad never grumbled about the cost of Ben's visits. This was because my father nurtured a secret dream left over from boyhood of being a cowboy. And Ben was as close to a cowboy as my father had ever seen. What he was doing in Maine, the farthest east one can possibly get in the United States, was a mystery, but here he was.

He showed up soon after breakfast one Saturday morning in September, and we all (including Melissa, of course) trooped out to say hello and round up the horses.

"Howdy," he called out as he unfolded his long, lean frame from the cab of his truck. Despite the chilly wind, he wore only a tight white T-shirt, a black hat, Wrangler jeans held up by a wide leather belt, and what he liked to call his pointed "roach-killing" Western boots.

He grabbed Mom and kissed her on the cheek and then pumped Dad's hand. "Hiya, ladies," he said with a cheery wave at Sharon, Melissa, and me. Then he opened his truck, got out his box of tools, and strapped on his chaps, all the while chatting away to Dad about this or that.

Still talking, he motioned Melissa to bring Really forward. He always started with Really, because he hated shoeing ponies. "It's heck on my back." He sighed and bent over to pick up a hoof. Really stood meekly. She had tangled with him just once, and when it was over, she'd ended up pinned to the barn floor beneath him. Ben hadn't been mean; he hadn't even gotten mad. He'd just matter-of-factly flipped her down and showed her that he was boss. How I wished I could do that.

When Really's shoes were removed and her hooves trimmed, Ben stretched his back, and I brought Sweetheart forward. "Hi there, old circus girl," Ben said, affectionately rubbing her neck. He placed a sugar lump on her nose, and she tossed it up and caught it. This was a trick she would perform only for him. "Tell me what you've been up to," he said as he bent over and picked up her hoof. She nuzzled his back fondly.

I stood holding her head, marveling at the way Ben could make our mismatched bunch seem like the greatest horses in the world. He had a talent not only for horseshoeing, but for bringing out the best in everyone, man or beast.

This was the first time that Ben had seen Fancy,

however, and he whistled when Dad led her up. "Whoo whee," he said. He ran a knowledgeable hand over her withers, inspected the scar over her left eye, and lifted one of her massive hooves. "You belong out on the prairies, my girl," he said, feeding her a carrot. "Bet you could go for miles and miles," he added.

"Fancy's trained to ride English and Western," Dad said proudly.

"English—nah!" Ben said as he placed a hoof between his legs and started to pull out the shoe nails. "She's a Western horse through and through." He was so calm and gentle that Fancy settled down and relaxed. This caused Ben a lot of trouble because as she dozed, she slowly leaned more and more on him until he was trying to hold her hoof and support all two thousand pounds of her.

"Straighten up!" he cried, elbowing her sharply, and Fancy snorted awake. But a few minutes later we could see her eyes flutter shut as she slouched downward yet again.

"Glad that's over," Ben said when all four of Fancy's humongous shoes were removed. He straightened up and wiped his sweaty face with the big red handkerchief he kept in his back pocket.

We let Fancy out into the paddock while Ben stiffly walked around, trying to work the kinks out of his back. "I bet she's one heck of a trail horse," he said. He was talking to Melissa and me, since Dad had gone to the house to fetch some coffee, and Sharon and Mom had wandered off. I sort of squirmed and looked at my feet as I muttered, "I only ride her in the ring."

Ben was too polite a guy to say it, but I knew he

was thinking *What a shame*. Instead he just leaned his arms on the fence and studied Fancy awhile.

Then he said, "You know, she's the spitting image of Matt Dillon's horse on *Gunsmoke*."

"What's *Gunsmoke*?" Melissa asked.

"Just the greatest Western show ever produced on TV," Ben answered as he knocked his hat back on his head with one arm.

"Matt Dillon was a U.S. Marshal based out of Dodge City, Kansas, during the wildest times in the West. He was always sorting out gunfights and riding after bandits. He had this great horse named Buck that could gallop for miles, jump fences, plunge down ravines, and even swim rivers."

Ben paused and then pointed at Fancy. "And he looked just like Fancy there."

"Was Matt Dillon's horse as big?" I asked.

"Oh yeah. Dillon was a large guy, and he needed a powerful horse. But he also needed one that would help him, and I'm sure Fancy's been trained to do that, too," Ben added.

Dad arrived with the coffee, and Ben and Dad started talking about the rising price of hay. Melissa climbed up on the fence beside me.

"Did you hear that?" she asked me.

"Mmm," I answered absently. To be honest, I'd suddenly had a vision of galloping Fancy through the tumbleweeds of the great Western prairie.

"We really ought to try and ride her outside," Melissa said, and my image instantly changed to a rattlesnake leaping out, Fancy spooking, and me landing headfirst on a cactus.

"Uh, I don't think so," I said.

Melissa would have kept arguing, only it started to rain, and we had to say a quick good-bye to Ben and run for cover. It didn't look like it was going to stop anytime soon, so we dashed down to Gramp's house, because he had an endless supply of sugared gumdrops, a big-screen TV, and two hundred channels to choose from. The only problem was that you had to watch whatever Gramp was watching, which sometimes meant boring old shows like *Wheel of Fortune*.

Today, however, we were lucky, because just as we arrived, there was an old Western movie starting, which promised lots of action for me and lots of horses for Melissa. We each grabbed a handful of gumdrops from Gramp and sprawled out on the threadbare (but genuine, as Mom always pointed out) Oriental carpet in front of the fire.

And on came Clint Eastwood with his poncho, a flat hat, and a tall horse. Lawrence of Arabia and Matt Dillon instantly faded into insignificance as Clint, the best-looking guy in the West, became my secret hero. I decided it was much more exciting to be the escaping bandit, galloping across the Western wilderness with one hand holding the reins and the other my hat, than to be a law-abiding member of the posse hot on my trail.

Well, okay, I could never be Clint, and my chances of heading West anytime soon were remote at best, but Ben had been correct in pointing out that I did possess a tall horse and a Western saddle. My mind teetered between the dream and the fear of actually doing it—riding Fancy outside of the ring.

Melissa sensed her advantage and pressed it.

"Just think what fun it would be," she whispered. "To canter across the Narrows together! Come on—let's try it tomorrow."

Caught up in the moment as I was, and feeling ashamed that Ben thought I was a yellow-bellied chicken, I let my common sense slither away and agreed.

But later on, reality settled in the pit of my stomach like the cold of the September night. And as I climbed into bed, I prayed that it would rain again tomorrow.

# 14

# Feats of Derring-Do OR Stuck in the Muck

**By now you've probably figured out that luck and I** do not get on too well together. So the next day, of course, dawned so clear that not a cloud could be found anywhere in the entire sky.

"Indian summer!" my mother cried, flinging open all the doors and letting the morning breeze off the ocean rush in.

My father coughed, enveloped in bacon smoke in the kitchen. "Sally!" he hollered. "I'm trying to cook breakfast here!"

Mom closed one door as a compromise and then helped me set the table, handing me five knives and forks.

"Hey, you gave me an extra one, Mom," I said, thinking she had miscounted.

"Aren't you and Melissa riding today?" Mom asked.

"Yes, but not until—"

There was a knock on the screen door and a familiar voice called, "Hello!"

Mom arched her eyebrows knowingly, and I shook my head. Sometimes I thought Mom and Melissa shared a telepathic power.

"Morning, Melissa," Dad said from the kitchen,

"what brings you around so early?"

Melissa laughed since it was completely obvious. She was wearing jodhpurs and riding boots.

"Have some breakfast," Mom offered, though the table was already set for five.

"Sure." Melissa grinned.

After I lingered over breakfast as long as possible, and Mom droned us full of instructions and orders about not riding out of sight, Melissa dragged me to the barn. We saddled Sweetheart first and then Fancy, who still required teamwork to get the saddle on her. We led both horses outside to the driveway and found Really pacing back and forth by the gate, eyes rolling, sides heaving, absolutely distraught over the thought of being left behind.

"Well," I said to her, "if you weren't such a meanie, you could be coming with us, too." I felt a satisfying sense of justice after all the years of torment.

Sweetheart preened and pranced around Fancy, full of pride that she had been the one chosen to accompany her. There was no coughing or limping today.

"She's full of it," I warned Melissa.

It was sunny, but the breeze off the ocean was cold, so we zipped up our jackets. Melissa helped shove me up onto Fancy and then climbed onto Sweetheart. We were ready.

I took a deep breath to steady my shaking hands and tried not to let my life flash in front of my eyes as we headed, once again, down the road toward the Narrows.

Gramp came running out with the camera. "Smile, girls!" he called, and we stopped to pose proudly.

"How I looked before the disfiguring accident," I muttered.

We rode across the Narrows and up the hill to the trees. After a short discussion that involved lots of persuading by Melissa, we ignored Mom's advice and disappeared into the woods of the Point.

At the farthest end we stopped and watched the boats steam by, heading into the Mainland boatyards for winter haul-up.

"We have to turn for home now," I announced nervously.

"Yup, this is it," Melissa said. Only she sounded excited. She turned first, as we had agreed earlier, in the hopes that Fancy would follow Sweetheart's lead. Sweetheart immediately began her prancing act.

I gulped a large breath and turned Fancy to follow her, and that is just what she did. Nothing happened—no tricks, no jumps, no bucking, nothing but a walk maybe a hair faster than normal.

"Hey," I called to Melissa, "look at this!"

Melissa looked, and so did Sweetheart, and the minute she realized she was leaving Fancy behind, the queen of preen herself dropped back to a walk alongside Fancy. She pretended that this was the way she always acted, although she couldn't resist an occasional jump and sideways hop.

We walked and trotted around the Point again and then crossed the Narrows.

"Let's canter back to the woods," Melissa suggested as we stopped at the end of the Narrows.

"I don't know," I said uncertainly. Things had gone well so far, but maybe we shouldn't overdo it, I thought.

"Just across the Narrows and up the hill," Melissa said. "Nice and slow. Fancy's behaving beautifully; she won't try anything."

"Well . . ." I still hesitated. It *would* be fun, the two of us cantering along together. "Okay," I said, ignoring the tiny voice in my head that screamed *Don't do it!* "Just to the top of the hill—you go first, and I'll follow."

Melissa quickly turned Sweetheart around before I could change my mind—she knew I would if I had another minute to think it over. She nudged Sweetheart into a slow canter, and Fancy and I followed. Then Sweetheart flew ahead, and Fancy picked up speed until we were just behind her. Fancy's gait was jarring as usual, but I hung on to the pommel with my free hand. We bounced along, the salt breeze blowing my hair in my face, and I tried to find a comfortable place on the hard saddle.

Sweetheart jumped over a little pile of seaweed in a smooth leap, and I gripped the pommel harder, waiting for the inevitable jolt as Fancy prepared to jump it also. But when it came, it was more than I bargained for. She caught her hoof and stumbled. Down went her neck. One rein was jerked out of my hand and I fell forward, the pommel catching me in the gut. Then Fancy caught herself, and up we rose again. She lunged after Sweetheart as I fell back in the saddle. I would have rolled completely off if it wasn't for that blessed pommel, which I was still gripping.

The one free rein whipped around wildly. "Whooaahhh," I cried, trying to stop her by pressing the other rein against her neck.

I honestly believe that Fancy didn't intend to do what happened next. It was just that the flapping rein, the sudden "whoa" command, and the one rein I still held tight confused her. Responding to it, she suddenly veered left off the road and onto the beach, pounded over the sand and straight out onto the mudflats. The tide was out, so she plunged farther and farther out into the mud. With each lunge I bounced clear off the saddle. I lost both stirrups, dropped the other rein, and clung to the pommel with both hands while muck and water flew everywhere.

"Wh . . . oo . . . ah! Wh . . . ooo . . . aahhh!" I finally managed to cry again. Fancy immediately jerked to a stop, and I shot forward over her neck and slithered down her muddy legs. *Spluck!* I hit the cold mud, and then there was silence except for the seagulls, whose lunch we had interrupted.

I sat up, dazed, and looked around. Fancy stood beside me, head down, sides heaving, all four legs deep in the mud.

"Sophie!" Melissa called from the beach, and I turned to see her frantically waving as she tumbled off a startled-looking Sweetheart.

I lifted my hand to wave and felt a stabbing pain. I glanced down at my hand. It looked okay, but it hurt like heck to move.

Now I'd done it, I thought with some surprise. After all these years, I'd finally gone and broken something while riding a horse, as I'd always predicted I would.

I scrambled to my feet, and Fancy swung her head around as if to say *Why did you lead me out here?* She was completely covered in blobs of black-brown mud and looked like an overgrown black and tan Dalmatian. I grabbed the muddy reins and slowly pulled her around with my good hand.

"Come on, girl," I coaxed, and she heaved forward, sucking each massive hoof out of the mud carefully. Together we plodded back toward the shore, where Melissa and Sweetheart waited anxiously on the beach.

"You okay?" Melissa asked when we finally emerged up onto the sand.

"I think I broke my wrist," I said, clutching it to my chest.

"Really?" Melissa's eyes popped wide open, but she kept on talking. "You should have seen that run. It was wild! What happened?"

"We just discovered that Fancy doesn't jump," I said.

∩ ∩ ∩

My tragically broken wrist turned out to be a slight sprain, but as it warranted a trip to the doctor in town and I returned sporting a bona fide bandage, I felt adequately traumatized.

Sharon was less than sympathetic since she had to hose off Fancy, oil her tack, and then clean the barn. When Sharon finally came in, she refused to even look at me, lying on the couch in the living room. She stomped by on the way to her room. That was a pain I decided I could bear.

Melissa, good sport as ever, had helped Sharon, though she didn't receive any thanks. She came in and sat beside me.

"Why do these things always happen to me?" I whined. I hadn't cried, but it was true and so depressing.

"It was just bad luck. How were we to know she's

a lousy jumper? She tried to do what you asked her to do," Melissa said, loyally defending Fancy.

I shrugged indifferently.

"You should have seen her dashing straight onto those mudflats, water and muck flying everywhere, and you hanging on through it all! It was better than either *Lawrence of Arabia* or Clint Eastwood," Melissa added.

"Oh?" I said, perking up.

"And she stayed right by you," Melissa concluded.

"She was stuck in the mud," I pointed out.

"Still—she didn't panic. Sweetheart would have made such a scene, she would have broken a leg," Melissa said.

"That's true," I agreed.

"Sophie, you aren't going to stop riding her, are you?" Melissa asked. She said it casually, but I knew she was holding her breath for the answer.

I lay on the couch thinking it over. My body ached, my wrist throbbed, and I kept having nasty little fear-filled flashbacks. But in between those, I remembered the nice ride around the Point and how Fancy had done absolutely everything I had asked her to do without complaint.

Melissa was right; Fancy hadn't done it on purpose.

"Yes, I'm still going to ride her," I said, and Melissa broke out in a great grin. I smiled and shook my head in disbelief. I was turning out to be no better than all the other dreamy-eyed girls I scorned.

# 15

# Running Unbridled OR The Night of the Halloween Horse

**The pain and the fear seemed almost worthwhile,** given the celebrity status I gained in school from my accident. Melissa was allowed to sit beside me in all our classes (normally we were kept separate due to excessive talking), because I needed help writing. I had to repeat the story several times for people, and news really spread when Melissa brought in her copy of Gramp's picture of us riding together. Even the boys had something good to say when they saw the size of Fancy and heard how I had stayed on her until the very end.

Susan, naturally, ignored me, and Heidi certainly wasn't about to look me in the eye. But that didn't concern me. It was Rachel's lack of sympathy that had me worried. I knew it was because Melissa had shared the adventure with me.

During lunch I slipped into the library where she sat reading.

"Hi," I whispered, sliding into a seat beside her.

"Why, if it isn't Calamity Jane," Rachel said, but she added a smile.

I breathed a sigh of relief. "You want to go to the mall Saturday?" I asked. "Mom said I could bring a friend."

"What about Melissa?" Rachel asked pointedly.

"She doesn't like shopping," I admitted, then quickly added, "besides, I want to go with you."

Melissa wasn't pleased when I told her on the bus ride home.

"I can't ride anyway," I pointed out.

She shrugged and stared out the window.

"Aw, come on, Melissa—come shopping with us. It'll be fun," I said.

Melissa wrinkled her nose. "Shopping? Fun? *No way!*"

∩ ∩ ∩

After two weeks had passed, the doctor pronounced me unbelievably fit and said I could ride again. However, it was now October and getting colder by the day, so our rides grew shorter and shorter.

Halloween was approaching and also the day following it—my birthday. Rachel asked me to go trick-or-treating with her and agreed to come out to the Island. Melissa assumed that we were, as usual, going trick-or-treating together after the Island Hall party.

So, there I was, caught in a dilemma and not knowing what to do. I had gone from having no friends to having two, neither of whom I wanted to lose. Finally, when Halloween was only a week away, I broke down and told Melissa. We had just finished a quick ride around the Point, but the wind was so cold that even she didn't suggest continuing on. I was cleaning stalls while Melissa cut open the hay bales.

"I know what I want for my birthday," I announced.

"Yeah, what?" Melissa asked, tugging at a bale.

"I want you to try and be friends with Rachel," I said, busily forking manure into the wheelbarrow.

Melissa stopped and straightened up. "That is just about the stupidest thing you've ever said," she declared, hands on hips.

I shrugged and went on cleaning the stall.

"I mean, that's as silly as asking me to single-handedly go out and save the whales or something," Melissa said in disgust.

"Well, that's what I want," I said stubbornly.

Melissa snorted. "Look, if you want me to hang out with Rachel, fine, but don't give up a birthday present. What a waste!" She went back to flaking out the hay bale.

"In that case," I said quickly, "I want a hat like Clint Eastwood's, and Rachel is coming trick-or-treating with us next week."

*"Geez Louise,"* Melissa said, shaking her head.

But, to my amazement, she stuck to her word and actually tried to be pleasant. Rachel sat with us at lunch, and we planned our costumes. The cold weather ruled out our being cavewomen or mermaids and, since the Island was one by three miles long, that ruled out any costumes we couldn't easily walk in. Also, the fact that we were now in seventh grade meant that we had to come up with something cool or at least scary.

∩ ∩ ∩

For three days we bounced ideas around, but at last we gave up on being original and decided to go as three witch sisters. Melissa and Rachel agreed to spend the night, partly because the next day was my birthday and partly because Mom was the best (and only) makeup artist around. I was feeling pretty pleased about life. True, Rachel and Melissa circled each other like wary cats, but overall, things weren't going too badly.

On Halloween night, Rachel came home on the bus with us. We all rushed out to clean the barn and let the horses in, and then we ran back inside to gulp down dinner and get ready. Mom had already made three crooked, bumpy noses out of papier-mâché. We each had a black robe and a wig. Mom painted Melissa's face puke green, Rachel's a pussy shade of yellow, and mine pure white with a red scar running down one cheek.

"Your latest riding accident," Melissa joked.

"Ha-ha," I said, putting on my tall, pointed hat.

Mom gathered us together and added a few warts here and there, and then we were ready. We all laughed when we looked in the mirror. Dad snapped a picture and then drove us up to the Hall. After going to the party, we would go trick-or-treating. We had to be home by ten o'clock.

I would have ignored this curfew, as my mother would never be able to stay awake, but it was Dad who had issued the command. And since my sister had to be in by eleven o'clock and was openly protesting, I knew he was going to be up watching both the TV and the clock. But still, we'd have plenty of time to party and gather candy—and to carry out my secret plan to toilet paper old Mrs. Pelletier's garden.

Last spring, Sweetheart had cleverly worked open the paddock gate latch, and all three horses had gotten loose. Led by Sweetheart, they had proceeded to go on a wild rampage up-island. Most people were forgiving and understanding, but not Mrs. Pelletier. That mean old bat made Sharon and me work all of one Saturday—pruning, weeding, and clearing her garden, and doing far more work than the damage our horses had ever caused. And then she hadn't even thanked us.

Sharon had shrugged, said, "Nasty old bird!" and returned to dreaming about her latest boyfriend, but my heart was filled with the need for retribution. And tonight, I informed my partners-in-crime-to-be, was the night.

First, however, we roamed around the Hall party helping the younger kids bob for apples and play musical chairs—being far too old ourselves, of course, to join in those silly games anymore. And then we set off for the middle of the Island, where most of the houses sat clustered together and the candy pickings were good. When our bags were bulging and we had stuffed ourselves full of chocolate, we set out for old Mrs. Pelletier's house.

She lived at the end of a short street off the main road. There were other houses, but hers was last and surrounded by the woods. Perfect cover. We snuck around the back of her house and left our bags and hats behind a big oak tree.

"Okay," I whispered as I handed Rachel and Melissa each a roll of toilet paper, "the garden's on the left, toward the road. Rachel, you do the crab-apple tree; Melissa, you take the rosebushes; and I'll do the rest."

We crept closer. Mrs. Pelletier's house was completely dark. She didn't believe in giving candy away to the “spoiled children of today.”

Stifling giggles, we moved into action. Rachel wound her roll around and around the tree, and Melissa and I crisscrossed each other, trying not to laugh when we bumped into each other in the dark and fell over. We had just picked ourselves up after one of those crashes when we heard the wail of a siren.

My body froze in place as blue lights appeared at the top of the street.

“The police!” Melissa gasped.

“Run!” Rachel hissed, and dropping her roll, tore past us for the woods. Melissa grabbed my hand and jerked me along with her as the headlights of the car swung down onto Mrs. Pelletier’s road. I stumbled over my robe, snatched it up in one hand, and ran as fast as I could into the woods. We all met behind the big oak and huddled down on the cold ground, trembling.

*“Geez Louise! Geez Louise!”* Melissa kept whispering over and over.

“Shhh!” Rachel hissed.

I held my hand over my heart to try and stop its pounding as the police car rolled to a stop. Two officers climbed out and walked up to Mrs. Pelletier’s porch. The lights clicked on inside the house, and Mrs. Pelletier opened the door.

The three of them held some sort of conversation that we couldn’t hear, and then Mrs. Pelletier glanced toward her garden and let out a shriek that we definitely could hear. She waved her arms wildly and then wagged a finger in the officer’s faces.

“I think she’s yelling at them,” Rachel whispered.

“We’re in for it now,” Melissa said, her normally confident voice wobbling.

I still couldn't speak.

Mrs. Pelletier stomped back inside and slammed the door. The two officers looked at each other, shook their heads, and headed for the car. I sighed in relief but then sucked all the air back in when one of them pulled a large flashlight out of the car and beamed it at the woods.

"Duck!" I hissed, and we scrunched down even lower behind the tree. The light swung closer and closer and then stopped at the oak tree for what seemed like hours before it moved to the right.

"I don't see anything, Charlie," the one with the flashlight called out to his partner, who was walking up the road. He switched off the light, got into the car, and drove up the street to the next house.

Rachel and Melissa and I let out our breath. My legs and arms felt like jelly as we watched the two policemen stop and talk to people in every single house on the street. Then they hopped back in the car, switched on the blue lights again, and disappeared up the Island.

I collapsed against the tree, sweaty and cold.

*"Geez Louise!"* Melissa said yet again.

"That was *close*." Rachel whistled between her teeth.

"Let's get out of here!" I said, and we got stiffly to our feet.

We couldn't go up the road since everyone had been alerted to our crime, so we took the path through the woods that led to the old Tinker farm. As soon as we were away from the lights of Mrs. Pelletier's street, we relaxed a little and began to laugh in relief.

"Well, they may have come close, but they didn't

catch us," Rachel pointed out. I couldn't see her face in the dark, but her voice sounded triumphant. I had to admire her. She had been the calmest and coolest among us.

"And they don't have any clues," Melissa added. We had made sure to take our hats and all of our candy with us.

"They'll never figure out who did it," I agreed. "Old Mrs. Pelletier's mean to everyone."

"Did you see the way she yelled at those cops?" Rachel said, and we burst into more giggles.

"Yeah, I bet they—" Melissa stopped talking, and then she stopped walking, and I plowed into her back.

"Ow!" Rachel said, bumping into me.

"Shhh!" Melissa said quickly.

"What is it?" I cried.

*"Listen!"* Melissa hissed.

At first all we could hear was the wind in the branches of the trees above us, but then came another noise. A noise of branches snapping. Something was coming up the path behind us, and whatever it was, was large and moving fast.

"Get off the path!" Melissa hollered, and we dove into the trees, bags of candy and hats forgotten.

The noise grew louder and closer, and my throat closed up. I suddenly remembered that it was Halloween, the night of ghosts and unexplained happenings. And then I heard another noise—the sound of thundering hooves. A dark shape loomed into sight, and I could hear the boom of labored breathing as it flew by, running with all its might. My fear faded into astonishment and then concern. I leaped up and jumped into the path.

"That was Fancy!" I cried. "She's gotten loose."

Rachel and Melissa clambered back onto the path beside me.

"Thank goodness. I thought it was a ghost." Rachel sighed in relief.

"How did she get out? Where are the others?" Melissa wanted to know.

"I don't know, but we have to try and catch her!" I said, starting up the path. "Did you see how fast she was going? She's probably scared to death, poor thing!"

Rachel and Melissa stopped to pile the candy and the hats under a tree, and then they caught up with me on the path. It was too dark to run, but after a few minutes, we burst out of the woods into Tinker's field. The moon was only half visible in the clouds, but as I scanned the field, I could just make out a large, dark shape standing at the upper end.

"There she is," I whispered and pointed.

Down at the other end stood Tinker's old abandoned barn. The roof was half off and it swayed to one side, but it was standing and had a door that still latched.

"We'll drive her down to the barn," I decided.

"I'm not getting anywhere near that horse," Rachel announced firmly.

"You go down and open the door, then," I said. "Melissa and I will go up either side of the field and herd her down toward you."

"Don't let her see you, or she'll spook and go for the woods," Melissa added. Now that she knew she wasn't going to be attacked by a ghost or arrested by the police, she was back to her usual confident self. Which was good, because my knees were still shaking.

We waited until we heard the creak of the old barn door opening. Fancy's dark head swung up sharply at the noise.

"Go!" I ordered, and Melissa and I split up. I crept up one side of the field, sticking close to the trees. Slowly I circled around and came closer and closer to Fancy, who remained alert and listening. I was just getting close enough to see her clearly when she suddenly bolted. I jumped up and waved my arms, and so did Melissa on the other side. Fancy zigzagged back and forth between us and then ran down toward the barn. Melissa and I ran after her, but she quickly left us far behind. At the last minute she swerved to the left, circled the barn, and headed back up the field.

"Close in!" I yelled to Melissa, and we ran toward each other, waving our arms. But the minute she saw us, Fancy dashed into the trees and disappeared from sight. A tremendous crackling and crashing echoed from the woods as she continued to run, the sound slowly getting farther and farther away.

"We've got to get Dad," I said as Rachel came running up. "Come on!"

We walked as fast as we could up Tinker's overgrown driveway to the main road. We turned for home, planning to flag down the first car that came along. But there was no traffic. We walked along for five minutes before Melissa said, "It's wicked quiet."

"Yeah, no cars, no kids, nobody," Rachel whispered.

We walked a little closer to each other. Except for the wind, it was silent and dark and eerie. We reached the top of my road, but that didn't make me feel any better; now we had to walk a mile in complete darkness on a lane with no streetlights and only three houses. Nervously, we started forward, not one of us daring to say how scared we were. And then headlights swept around the corner and a truck screeched to a halt beside us.

"Sophie?" a voice called.

"Dad!" I cried in relief, and we all ran for the truck.

"Thank goodness! I've been so worried," Dad said as he stepped out.

"We found her, Dad. She's up-island. We tried to drive her into Tinker's old barn, but she escaped into the woods," I said in a rush.

*"You what?"* Dad cried.

"I know she's scared, but we had to try," I explained. His expression, reflected in the headlights of the truck, was one of disbelief.

"Are you girls nuts? You could have been killed!"

"But Dad . . ." At that moment, blue lights appeared behind us, and my stomach twisted into a knot.

"Uh-oh," Rachel murmured.

"You found them?" one of the officers called out.

"Yes, thanks," Dad answered. "Okay, girls, hop in. We're going home."

"Home?" I cried. "But, Dad, we have to find her! Are the others okay? How did she get out?"

"How did who get out?" my father asked.

"What do you mean *who*?" I said impatiently.

Dad raised his arm to shield his eyes from the glare of the headlights as he peered at me in confusion. "What are you talking about?" he asked.

"What are *you* talking about?" I demanded.

"About the moose that swam to the Island," Dad said in an exasperated tone.

There was a moment of astonished silence.

Rachel and Melissa and I all looked at each other.

"Moose?" I finally said in a tiny voice.

∩ ∩ ∩

Later, after hot chocolate and at least two hours had passed, we were able to laugh and talk about everything that had happened.

"I can't believe it. The cops weren't after us at all—they were only warning folks about the moose," Rachel said. "How could we have been so stupid?"

"It sure seemed like they were after us," I said. I still felt queasy when I remembered those blue lights flashing. So much for my life of crime.

"A moose," said Melissa, shaking her head. "I still can't believe I ran around a field chasing a wild moose."

The next morning a policeman came to tell us that the game warden had shot the moose with a tranquilizer, and that she was being transported upstate to be released deep in the woods of Baxter State Park. We walked up-island and found our witch hats and our candy, and when we returned home, a newspaper reporter was waiting to interview us about what happened. We told the story we had worked out—making sure not to mention that we were anywhere near old Mrs. Pelletier's house, just in case.

We became minor celebrities on the Island and in school when the story about our attempt to capture a wild moose appeared in the town paper.

And finally, Rachel and Melissa became friends. I wouldn't say that they were the best of friends, but there is nothing like being scared to death twice in one night to create a bond between people.

And Fancy gained a new nickname also. Forever after that, everyone called her "that Moose Horse," and we affectionately called her "Moosie."

# 16

# Left at Home Alone OR One Short Ride in April

**Winter settled onto Maine once again. Snow fell,** freezing rain pelted down, and then there was such a cold snap that the water pipe froze in the new barn. We had to lug water from the house two times a day. The more I lugged, the more the horses seemed to drink.

It was so cold that sometimes we kept them in their stalls, which meant more horse-puckeys to clean out and more hay to heave down from above, as they ate both to stay warm and because they were bored. Dad grumbled about us running out of hay before winter ended.

Sweetheart figured out a way to open her door with her teeth, got out one day, and went on an eating binge in the grain box. But the vet came out and said she was okay. After we chained her door shut, Sweetheart leaned over to Fancy's door and undid her latch. Then Fancy got out and ate half the apples in the barrel. The vet came again, but said she was so large, her intestines could handle the intake. Dad wrote another check and said that *his* intestines were the ones we should be worried about. The vet laughed and slapped a sympathetic hand on Dad's shoulder.

The only bright spot was our weekly riding lessons. Rachel had decided she would rather take piano lessons, so it was still Melissa and me. It was cold in the ring, but the lessons were only half an hour in the winter, and the horses actually behaved better in the cold.

So with Melissa I rode, and with Rachel I continued to gossip and shop. Only now Melissa was included, which was progress, and it made sleepovers more fun because Melissa could always think up something fun and different to do. And when we weren't hanging out with Rachel, Melissa and I spent hours planning our summer riding schedule.

Slowly, the winter melted away, until at last it was April first. The snow had finally disappeared into the ground. What was left was mud. The horses were muddy; the trails were muddy; the driveway was muddy; in fact, the whole Island was awash in mud. But to see bare ground was still heartening, and as I walked to the bus stop, I thought happily about April vacation. Rachel was going to Florida to see her grandmother, but Melissa and I had planned to start riding, even if we had to wear splash guards.

Melissa came running up, late as always, as the bus swung into view and slowed to a stop in front of us. Sharon climbed on first, and I followed behind Melissa and settled into our seat.

"Want a peanut?" she asked, offering me the can.

"Forget it, Melissa—you try that trick every year," I scoffed, knowing full well about the fake snake that would spring out of the can.

Melissa looked around the bus. "And every year I find a new victim," she whispered. Straightening up, she turned and smiled at little Timmy Ross.

"Hey, want a peanut?" she offered.

"Sure." Timmy shrugged and opened the lid. The fake snake sprang out, hit him square in the nose, and then shot up to the ceiling of the bus. Timmy screamed, the girl beside him screamed, and then everyone on the bus screamed, thinking something terrible had happened.

Mr. Myers pulled the bus over to the side of the road. "What's going on?" he hollered.

Melissa grabbed the can and the snake and guiltily went forward to explain. "Please, Mr. Myers. It's April Fool's Day. I didn't know Timmy was going to scream like that," she pleaded.

"You didn't think he'd scream when a snake jumped out at him?" Mr. Myers asked.

"No . . . Yes . . . I mean, I didn't think about it," Melissa said, hanging her head. She looked extremely sorry.

Mr. Myers sighed. He jerked his thumb toward our seat. "Get back and sit down," he growled, "but if I hear one little peep out of you for the remainder of this bus ride. . . ." He left the threat hanging in the air unsaid, but Melissa understood perfectly.

"Thank you, Mr. Myers," she said, slinking back to our seat. The older kids snickered, but Melissa ignored them.

"Whew! That was close," she said, stuffing the snake back into the can and jamming it into her backpack.

"Stupid!" Timmy hissed from behind us.

"You're the stupid one; you opened the can," Melissa reminded him, and Timmy shut up.

"You'd better watch it with your tricks today," I said, shaking my head.

"I certainly will," Melissa replied with an evil grin.

At school I saw her and Rachel whispering together and thought they were planning to play a trick on me. I was very careful at lunch, but nothing happened. And nothing happened in science class or on the bus ride home. When we were only minutes from our bus stop, I couldn't stand the suspense any longer.

"Okay, Melissa, what gives?" I demanded. "It's April Fool's Day, and you haven't played one trick on me."

Melissa grinned. "Yet," she said, but then her smile faded. "It's because I have to tell you something, and it's not good news," she added.

I didn't like her serious expression. Melissa was never serious, and it meant that what she had to tell me *was*.

"Well, tell me!" I said impatiently.

"I'm going to Florida for April vacation," she blurted out as the bus pulled up to our stop.

"Oh," I said. I was disappointed, but I had thought she was going to tell me something positively awful. "Well, it could be worse," I said, shrugging.

The bus stopped, and Melissa grabbed her backpack. "With Rachel," she added quickly. Then she shot off the bus and ran down the road before I had a chance to say a word.

Not that there was anything to say.

I started the mile walk down to my house. Sharon had invited a friend over, so I walked very slowly until they disappeared around a bend ahead of me. Then I let my shoulders slump.

*Of all the rotten things to do*, I thought, kicking at a stone. So much for loyalty and friendship. I mean, I had to force them to even speak to each other in the beginning.

I was so angry I wanted to break something, but after a half mile, my anger deflated like a balloon. I wondered sadly why no one had asked me to go.

Rachel called me the minute I got home.

"So you and Melissa are going to Florida together?" I said bluntly.

"Didn't Melissa explain?" Rachel asked.

"She didn't need to. It seems pretty clear to me," I said, ready to hang up.

"Wait! Listen," Rachel insisted.

"Okay." I sighed and listened halfheartedly while Rachel explained. When her mom had found out Melissa's family was going to Florida, too, and flying into the same airport as Rachel, she arranged for Rachel to fly with them. That way Rachel wouldn't have to travel alone. It was just a coincidence that they were going to be in the same city together.

I felt a little better knowing that. They each insisted that they wished more than anything that I was going, too, but it was still hard not to be depressed when I heard them making plans to go to the beach together.

April didn't improve much after that. First, there was another cold spell, and then after that, a snowstorm—but it was on a Saturday, so we didn't even get to miss a day of school. Then Mom cheerfully announced that the Carpwells would be coming to visit the last weekend of our vacation.

To top it all off, the first day of vacation dawned sunny, the sky that robin's egg blue that meant the arrival of warm weather at last. I looked out the window at the sea of brown mud steaming in the sun and felt lost. It seemed everyone in the world had something to do and someone to do it with, except for me. My grandfather was away on a trip with Bob Estabrook, my parents had gone shopping, and Sharon and her new best friend, whom she changed as often as her clothes, sat downstairs watching TV and cackling at each other like hens.

The three horses stood together on the manure mound in the middle of the paddock. They were a sight to behold, with their thick winter coats covered in patches of mud and their manes all knotted with clumps. They faced the sun, dozing, eyes closed. I looked at them, sighed, and then felt disgusted with myself.

"Snap out of it!" I said out loud. I needed to do something.

I decided to go for a ride, the first one of the spring. I changed into my old jodhpurs and a holey sweater, pulled on my boots and a windbreaker, lined my pockets with sugar lumps, and slipped outside.

The sun did feel nice, and I breathed in the warm air deeply. Maybe it wasn't such a bad day after all.

I almost chose to ride Sweetheart, since a nice, smooth canter was appealing—but the thought of jouncing and prancing all the way home was not, so I approached Fancy instead. She didn't appreciate being woken from her nap, but easygoing sport that she was, she followed me into the stall with only four sugar lumps as incentive.

By now I could just manage to saddle her myself and knew how to get my foot into the stirrup and swing up quickly. It took only two tries before I was firmly in the saddle, and we were off. I decided against going up-island, since it was covered in April mud, and headed for the Point instead.

Fancy had really woken up by now and was tossing her head around, full of spring energy. I felt her enthusiasm and thought, *Why not? Let her run.* It would cheer me up, too. So halfway down the road to the Narrows, I stopped holding her back, and she lunged into her familiar walloping canter. We zoomed along in the wind, and I lifted one hand in the air. Faster and faster we flew along—and then I *was* flying through the air, still in the saddle but without the horse, arcing downward, until I crashed into the sea grass.

I lay there stunned, still clutching the pommel of the saddle, which I was sprawled across. Hot breath fanned my face, and I looked up to see Fancy peering down at me with an expression of curious concern.

I sat up and slowly felt all my bones. Nope, nothing broken. I moved off the saddle, inspected it, and found the problem. The old leather girth had snapped clean in two. It hadn't been oiled all winter, and I hadn't thought to check it before I saddled Fancy. It was my own fault I had a sore neck.

I stood up and looked around, but there was not a soul to see what had happened or to come help.

"Come on," I said to Fancy, who patiently stepped closer. I lifted up the saddle blanket and then the heavy saddle. For once, she didn't shy away when I hoisted it awkwardly onto her back.

"That's the problem with riding alone." I sighed as I adjusted it. "There's no one to help when you're in trouble." I gathered up the reins and looped them loosely around the pommel. I didn't need them, since Fancy always followed.

"No one to walk home with," I said as I started up the Narrows, and she plodded along beside me. "Or to make you feel better." We walked past Gramp's closed-up house, leaving hoof and boot prints on the wet lawn. "Or to say, *Hey! Stop whining, it's a beautiful day*." Fancy rubbed her head against my arm, nearly knocking me over.

We walked up the road and turned into the driveway of the barn. "Or to laugh at what a sight it must have been, me flying through the air on a saddle with no horse." I allowed myself a small chuckle, and Fancy snorted. I walked up the ramp and into her stall. She stomped along behind and shoved me aside.

"Or to listen to me talk about nothing," I said, lifting the saddle off her back and swinging it onto the stall door. Fancy cocked her ears forward and blew hot air in my ear. "Stop that!" I giggled, pushing her head away.

"Or who doesn't care that I'm not all that brave or brainy," I said, lifting the bridle off her head. Fancy obediently opened her mouth to let the bit slip out. "Or that I'm not at all popular," I admitted with another sigh. She lowered her head and nibbled at my pants pocket, and I fished out a sugar lump for her.

"And probably never will be," I added as she crunched away and followed me down the ramp and into the paddock. "But I guess that sometimes you just have to enjoy being all alone," I said, opening the gate. I patted Fancy on the neck and shooed Sweetheart and Really away from the opening.

Fancy waited, one eye following my every movement. I flicked my fingers.

"Go on, go and roll," I said. She tossed her head at me and trotted off. I watched her circle and then drop and roll back and forth, all four feet waving in the air. Really immediately copied her, though she was far too fat to roll over completely. Sweetheart stood watching by the gate, too much the princess to allow herself a roll in the mud.

She nudged me for sugar instead. I tickled her lip and made her laugh. Then I scratched her neck, and she arched it in pleasure.

"Nope," I said, "friends are tricky. You have to need them, and you have to not need them. You know what I mean, Sweetheart?" I asked. And, as we both looked over at Really and Fancy, who were now touching noses, I thought that maybe she did.

# Epilogue OR Ending

**Well, that's my story to date. I wish I could say that** I became an equine goddess and rode off into never-never land on a horse to live happily ever after, but I haven't.

The truth is that Really still likes to try and take a chunk out of me, Sweetheart manages to knock me off under a tree branch now and again, and Fancy, my loyal sidekick—well, I always have to be awake when I'm riding her, because she'd jump off the bridge to the Mainland if I didn't stop her.

I have come a long way with riding lessons, but just the other day when we were doing emergency dismounts, my foot got caught in the stirrup. I ended up facefirst in the sawdust, and Mr. Richards had to help me disentangle myself from the horse. I was so embarrassed. Things like that are only supposed to happen to beginners, but you know my luck.

Still, as a whole, things are looking up. I continue to live in fear of the Carpwells, but fortunately they're too busy with their farm to come visit often. And this summer I'm planning to teach riding lessons with Sweetheart-in-the-Ring. As part of the lesson, the kids have to clean the tack, brush the horse, and clean out a stall—and I get paid for it. Not a bad plan, eh?

I'm starting eighth grade this fall, but I don't think it will be too bad now that Rachel and Melissa and I are all pals. They returned from Florida more buddy-buddy than ever, so I guess I got my birthday wish. I had to adjust to the idea that I wasn't the center of things, but as it is now, Melissa and I do things together, Rachel and I do things together, we all do things together, and sometimes Rachel and Melissa do things without me.

And sometimes I like that, just being by myself.

At other times, I will admit, I slip out to the barn and into Fancy's or Sweetheart's or even Really's stall (if I have plenty of sugar). I press against them for warmth, and they let me do it—and with no one around except for the barn cats, I'll talk to them, and they'll listen, one ear cocked back.

The truth is, horses are nothing but trouble—but just when you've about had it with their shenanigans, you realize that they've somehow gone and become your friends, and you're stuck caring about them. So, if you think you love horses—and you still love them after reading this story—then I say go ahead: take the plunge and learn to ride.

But don't say I didn't warn you. . . .

## About THE Author

**Sarah P. Gibson** grew up on an island in Maine. In addition to enduring the agonies of owning a motley trio of horses and trying to make friends, Ms. Gibson also feared sailing tippy boats and skiing down icy mountains. Her love of reading and hatred of math led her to become a librarian, and being stuck on a small island made her yearn to travel. After visiting twenty countries and living in six, she is now back on the island, where she lives with her husband and two children. Learn more about her at www.SarahPGibson.com.

## About THE Illustrator

**Glin Dibley** loves to surf when he's not busy drawing and painting children's books for all ages. His fun, quirky style can be seen in such novels as *The Stupendous Dodgeball Fiasco* by Janice Repka and picture books, such as *Tub-boo-boo* by Margie Palatini and *Kid Tea* by Elizabeth Ficocelli. He lives in Huntington Beach, California, with his wife and two daughters.

8034854R00095

Made in the USA
San Bernardino, CA
26 January 2014